"They saved me," said the ___ phins playing in the nearby ___ ___ know that must sound crazy, but—"

"Don't try to talk," Joseph told the girl as he helped her onto shore.

"I'm Teegan," she whispered, her voice raw. "Our ship went down—"

"Hey, Joseph! I found coconuts! See!"

Joseph turned to see his friend Fleetfeet approaching. When Teegan saw the *talking* Stegoceras, her face paled. Shuddering, she backed away.

Fleetfeet stopped. "Was it something I said? You don't like coconuts?" He cracked one of them open with his claws and held it out to her.

"It speaks," she whispered in disbelief. "The *lizard* speaks!"

VISIT THE EXCITING WORLD OF

IN THESE BOOKS:

Windchaser by Scott Ciencin

River Quest by John Vornholt

Hatchling by Midori Snyder

Lost City by Scott Ciencin

Sabertooth Mountain by John Vornholt

Thunder Falls by Scott Ciencin

AND COMING SOON:

Firestorm by Gene DeWeese

DINOTOPIA®
THUNDER FALLS

by Scott Ciencin

BULLSEYE BOOKS

Random House 🏠 New York

*The publisher's special thanks to
James Gurney and Dan Gurney
and Scott Usher*

*My thanks (words cannot convey) to one of the
greatest editors on the planet, Alice Alfonsi.
And again, my profound appreciation to Jim Gurney
for creating a world in which basic goodness not only has meaning—
it has a value far beyond any other.*
—S.C.

To my dearest angel, my wife Denise,
You fire my imagination and fill my days with wonder—
I love you, sweetheart.
—S.C.

SOME FAVORITE
DINOTOPIAN SAYINGS

"To have strong scales." = *To be tough, to have thick skin.*

"To roll out of the nest." = *To leave the island.*

"To crack through the shell." = *To pass into adolescence.*

"A rolled-up scroll." = *Someone whose behavior is puzzling or unpredictable.*

"Something is boiling in the pot." = *Something is brewing.*

"To look at someone from horn to tail." = *To look someone up and down.*

"To be in the horsetails." = *To be lost or overwhelmed.*

"To be in someone's scroll." = *To be in good with someone.*

"Sing and it will go away." = *Take your mind off your troubles.*

"Jolly-head." = *Amusing fellow.*

"Head-scratcher." = *Worry, problem, difficulty.*

"Breathe deep, seek peace." = *Farewell, peace be with you, take it easy.*

THUNDER FALLS

CHAPTER 1

Waterfall City

Joseph laughed as an icy spray covered his face and shoulders. His seashell gondola bobbed as it raced along the rapidly moving water.

Right behind Joseph, in a seashell gondola of his own, was Joseph's best friend.

Fleetfeet was a stocky, short-necked Stegoceras with a hard, domed-shaped head that he enjoyed butting like a mountain goat.

In one way or another, butting heads had become a regular pastime for these two friends.

"Getting tired yet?" Joseph teased.

"Ha!" cried the saurian in a squawky, parrot-like voice. "I'm more worried about you! Do you think that shell of yours can take it?"

Joseph grinned at Fleetfeet's words. The saurian

language was different from human speech—the writing, as well. But Joseph had been taught to understand his dinosaur friends as well as his human ones.

So far, this morning's exciting ride had taken the two from a rise behind the great library to a twisting path around the Aqua Stadium.

The gondolas they rode in were shaped to look like large seashells and each was specially fitted for steering.

Joseph wore a harness that was rigged in a special way to his rudder. This let him change his boat's direction by rolling his shoulders. It was quite a balancing act, and he loved every second of it.

His friend Fleetfeet had attached his rudder to his tail. One swish either way and Fleetfeet's boat would respond!

The rushing waters grew louder as the canal snaked to one side. Suddenly, they plunged down a sharp dip and approached a turning point. Both Joseph and Fleetfeet knew what was beyond that point: the dangerous white water of Lower Thunder Falls.

Joseph didn't let the canal's roar stop him. He hollered, loud enough to make his throat sore. "I've only butted the sides twice! You've done it three times! I'm winning!"

"What was that?" Fleetfeet called. "I can't hear you!"

Joseph frowned. He tried to yell louder.

"Sorry!" Fleetfeet called. "Can't understand!"

Finally, Joseph turned his head and shouted with all his strength back at his rival, "I'm winning, helmet-head!"

A bump jolted Joseph. In frustration, he realized that his turning had made the gondola strike one of the sides.

"Three to three!" Fleetfeet cried.

"You did that on purpose! No fair!" Joseph said, laughing. He looked ahead once more. "You could hear me the whole time."

"You know that old saying Steelgaze told us!" answered Fleetfeet. *"Fair is the advantage to those who possess it!"*

"We're tied now, claw-brother! But the Great Divide is coming up, and then the score will change."

"How?"

"I'm going to try for it!" yelled Joseph.

"You mean go past the point of no return?" asked Fleetfeet. "It's forbidden!"

"For hatchlings and children maybe!" Joseph shouted. "But *I'm* fourteen—and it's been at least that many years since *you've* been a new hatchling!"

They hit a few more bumps and turns before Fleetfeet spoke. "Well—you may *try* to take on Thunder Falls, but *I* will succeed!"

Joseph looked ahead to the churning waters and wondered how safe this really was. Navigating the treacherous reaches of Thunder Falls in crafts like these would be difficult. But he knew it was possible.

So what am I worried about?

They turned another corner, and suddenly the Great Divide was directly before them. The canal split into two branches.

Along the rocky wall they'd been following appeared a tunnel. A sign had been chiseled into the stone above the tunnel:

CHILDREN AND HATCHLINGS TO THE LEFT
ADULTS TO THE RIGHT

The left-hand path flowed directly into the tunnel, but the right-hand path—the *adult* path—snaked around the tunnel and down to the Cargo Chute. From there, the path led to the dangerous white water that flowed below the grand waterfall known as Thunder Falls.

Joseph watched as the choppy waters rose up. His mouth suddenly felt dry, and he swallowed hard. He wanted to take the right-hand path. He wanted to very badly.

Joseph tried to see himself taking on the Cargo Chute and then Lower Thunder Falls.

He knew this wasn't a *boy's* challenge but one suited for a man. All he had to do was roll his shoulders to the right and he would prove himself ready for the future. A future filled with endless excitement!

If only his mentor, Steelgaze, could see this!

He was almost there…almost there. All he had to do was lean to the right.

But suddenly, at the last possible second, Joseph leaned hard the other way. His gondola sailed into the darkened tunnel, away from the Cargo Chute and Lower Thunder Falls.

He had lost his nerve.

Breathing hard, he quickly looked back over his shoulder. He didn't even notice his gondola bumping the side again as he spotted Fleetfeet following him.

Good, he thought, relieved that his best friend hadn't beaten him. *Fleetfeet must have lost his nerve, too.*

As the water leveled out and began to rise, Joseph felt his gondola slowing. Phosphorescence from the ceiling helped him see the tunnel walls.

Using his oar, Joseph started to paddle the rest of the way toward an underground dock. A small fleet of seashell gondolas as well as some larger rafts were moored there.

Once a week, the seashell gondolas were carried up to the main level of Waterfall City, which was laced with canals. From a starting point behind the library, children took turns riding down through the chutes to the dock underground.

This morning, Joseph and Fleetfeet had arrived late at the library dock—only two gondolas had been left. The dock-master had urged them to take only one gondola, but they argued against it. Each of them wanted his own.

"Why?" the dock-master had asked them. "If you share one gondola, then Fleetfeet can take the rudder while Joseph works the front with an oar. That is the best way to work the boat."

Joseph and Fleetfeet gave their usual answer when told to work together: "Where's the fun in that?"

In a single craft, they would have no way to *compete* with one another. And challenging each other had been a way of life for them ever since they'd come into Steelgaze's care, eight years earlier.

Disappointment and an overwhelming sense of failure washed over Joseph as he took off his harness and guided his gondola to a small pier. All the other children and their guardians were already gone. The chamber was deserted except for the two of them.

As Joseph began tying off the mooring lines, Fleetfeet eased his gondola close.

"That was a smart move you made back there," Fleetfeet said.

"What do you mean?"

"Your harness was coming loose. If you hadn't turned when you did…"

For a moment, Joseph was confused. There'd been nothing wrong with his harness. Not that he'd noticed, anyway. Then he realized that his friend was just trying to make him feel better. *Well*, thought Joseph, *I don't need to be protected.*

"You have to be careful with these things," Joseph said, thrusting out his jaw. "Thunder Falls isn't going anywhere. It'll wait for us, don't you think?"

"Absolutely. I'd have gone ahead and taken the adult path myself, but I had to make sure you were all right. So I turned left."

"Yeah, thanks." Joseph shrugged. "Who won the game, anyway?"

"You banged the side once on the way into the tunnel," Fleetfeet said. "So I won, of course."

"Well, I don't know about the 'of course.' You either won or you didn't. We usually finish neck and neck."

"Sure," squawked Fleetfeet, dropping his head and butting it playfully into his friend's shoulder. "When I'm feeling generous enough to *let* you win."

An immediate reply rose up in Joseph, but he forced it down. Fleetfeet had been nice enough not to make an issue out of Joseph's sudden loss of nerve at the Great Divide. The least he could do was allow his friend to strut for a moment.

Besides, though they were each very serious about winning any and every competition, their taunts and silly banter were just part of the game.

Mostly.

Once they were done mooring the gondolas, Joseph and Fleetfeet sat back on the dock. Joseph took off his boots and let his feet dangle in the cool waters. Leaning back, he stared up at the murals covering the chamber's vast ceiling.

The images were of humans and dinosaurs working and playing together. Joseph and Fleetfeet knew that their fellow Dinotopians strongly believed in the idea of cooperation.

It had been that way for hundreds and hundreds of years. Ever since the first humans had become ship-wrecked on this isle of evolved dinosaurs.

Working together was how the two species were able to create the amazing canals of Waterfall City and the many other beautiful sites on Dinotopia.

Despite their constant competition, Joseph and Fleetfeet did believe in the Dinotopian way of life. The two knew they could always count on each other's friendship. The truth was, they were more than friends. Circumstances had made them brothers.

Joseph looked around the chamber. There was an air of faded elegance to the place. Some of the gondo-las were half-sunk. Others were decorated with chips of plaster fallen from the ceiling.

"What do you think this place was used for?" Joseph asked.

"Don't know." Fleetfeet was busy fiddling with the silver claw-buttons on his brightly colored vest. It was a prize from the first contest he'd ever played against an adult. He rarely took it off.

"I heard that once there was a whole other system of canals down here. Some went dry, others got over-filled and dangerous. Most of them were walled up."

"I believe that."

"Hey," Joseph said, sitting up again. "Speaking of

mysteries, I heard Lee Crabb was in Waterfall City."

"So?"

"He's just such a sourpuss. Always scheming. That's what people say."

The Stegoceras shook his head. "And you listen?"

"Well…"

Suddenly, footsteps sounded from behind them. Joseph and Fleetfeet turned to see a rugged-looking man approach. He was tall and bearded, dressed in subdued colors. He wore a purple velvet waistcoat, black leggings, and dark blue boots. His shirt was a faded crimson.

"Townsend!" Joseph cried. He was surprised to see his mentor's old friend. Townsend was the only name the man used.

"Boys, you must come home at once," Townsend said. He looked pained. His usually expressionless features were wrenched with sadness. "Something terrible has happened."

"Is it Steelgaze?" Fleetfeet asked.

Hopping to his feet, Joseph frantically slid on his boots. "Is he all right?"

"I'll explain when we get there. Come!" Townsend spun on his heels and walked quickly toward the spiral staircase at the far end of the chamber.

The boys hurried after him.

CHAPTER 2

Joseph and Fleetfeet rushed home. Townsend was right behind them.

The two boys gave no thought to the great piles of leaves left on the street, perfect for leaping into. They ignored the cries of other children to come join them in games. They didn't even consider the song of the fountain's waters, though they stopped there at least once a day.

Instead, they sped along until they came to a large house with double doors wide enough for its owner, a sixteen-foot-long Kentrosaurus, to pass through.

After Joseph and Fleetfeet entered the main hallway, Townsend turned to them. "Quiet now. Quiet. Don't make a fuss."

"Is he—" Joseph began, his voice tense.

Fleetfeet nodded frantically. "Is Steelgaze—"

"He's all right for the moment," Townsend said.

"In fact, he wants to see both of you."

"What happened?" asked Joseph.

Sadness came into Townsend's eyes. "I suppose I should tell you. Steelgaze certainly won't. There was a fire not far from here."

"I thought I smelled ash in the air," Fleetfeet said.

"What caught fire?" Joseph asked.

Townsend stopped and hugged himself. "A Hatchery."

Gasps came from Joseph and Fleetfeet.

"Steelgaze was on his way to the market," Townsend continued. "He rushed inside. The eggs and those who tended them in the incubation room had already been rescued, but a human child and two Ovinutrix were trapped on the second floor."

"No!" cried Joseph.

Fleetfeet placed a single claw on Joseph's shoulder. "We must have strong scales. Townsend, please go on."

The older man nodded. "The stairway had collapsed. Steelgaze rose up on his hind legs, using his tail for balance. The trio climbed down on his back, using his spikes the way others might use a stepladder. But the fire reached Steelgaze's exposed underbelly. He's in great pain. Several of those who tended the Hatchery are seeing to him."

Townsend gestured to a wide door just ahead. "He's in there."

Joseph darted for the door, but Townsend caught him.

"Wait," Townsend said. "I know how you feel about Steelgaze. When the floods claimed your parents, he became your only family." The older man turned to Fleetfeet. "And your story is equally sad. The loss of your people during the trek to Tentpole of the Sky—"

"That which is lost can be found again," Fleetfeet said, proudly straightening his saurian shoulders.

Joseph felt sorry for his friend. Fleetfeet's persistence was one of his best qualities—until it turned into blind stubbornness. He refused to be comforted on the loss of his family because he firmly believed that they would one day return for him.

"Yes," Townsend said softly. "I hope you're right."

"Hope has nothing to do with it," Fleetfeet said, automatically aiming his domed head at Townsend and shaking it, as if readying for battle. "That which is, is. There is nothing more to be said."

"Yes, there is." Townsend waited for Fleetfeet to look up again and then his penetrating gaze went back and forth between the two boys. "Now is the time to show Steelgaze that his lessons have taken root, that each of you is truly ready to crack through the shell. I know it would be a comfort to him."

"I would move sea and mountains for Steelgaze!" Joseph cried.

"As would I!" Fleetfeet joined in.

"Then," Townsend said, "act as if you are not worried. You know how he can be."

"Absolutely," Joseph said.

12

"Yes, yes," Fleetfeet said breathlessly. "Let us see him!"

The trio entered a spacious chamber where Steelgaze waited. The Kentrosaurus lay across a large resting chair.

At sixteen feet long and weighing close to two tons, Steelgaze had a small, lizard-like head compared to his massive almond-shaped body. A paired row of triangular bone plates ran from his neck to the midsection of his back. From there to the end of his thick tail, tall spikes protruded.

The chair's underside was mostly cut away so that his wounded belly could be tended. A golden shaft of light fell from the single window above. It shone upon two young women and a trio of Ovinutrix who were applying salves to his wounds and bandaging his underbelly.

A basket filled with leaves had been placed within his reach. But the food looked as if it hadn't been touched, which worried Joseph.

"Really, really, I don't see why you're making such a fuss," said the Kentrosaurus. "Tend to the eggs. I'm fine. Don't waste your time on me."

A fiery-haired woman patted his unburned flank. His red-brown scales glittered in the sunlight. "The eggs are being well tended. And *you* are hardly a waste of time!"

"I think he's cute!" one of the Ovinutrix said.

"He acts crabby, but he really loves the attention," teased the other.

Steelgaze turned and saw that his students had arrived. "Greetings, lads! Tell them what a thick hide I have! Tell them this isn't necessary!"

"Do nothing of the kind," Townsend said. "Now is hardly the time to indulge your teacher's tendency to drag his tail."

"Oh, and now I'm stubborn, too?" Steelgaze asked. He sighed deeply. "Am I to have no peace today?"

Joseph approached Steelgaze, tears welling in his eyes. "This is our fault, isn't it? If we'd been with you instead of off playing—"

"Don't be silly. How could you possibly have known?" Steelgaze asked. He angled his head in Townsend's direction. "Old friend, would you persuade my *keepers* here to give me a few moments alone with Joseph and Fleetfeet?" His tail swung idly from side to side.

"Your keepers!" one of the women exclaimed.

One of the Ovinutrix took her hand. "Come, Leonora. Don't let old jolly-head here get to you. He's only teasing."

"How do you know?" asked Leonora.

The ostrich-sized saurian laughed. "I know his type. All hoot and no horn. Besides, look at his tail. He always does that when he's being playful."

Steelgaze's tail froze in mid-swipe. "Humph."

The women laughed. One of them kissed Steelgaze's head.

"Fah!" he cried. "Away! Away!"

Grinning, Townsend escorted them from the chamber.

"Now, both of you come closer," Steelgaze said. "I'm not going to bite. I don't have the strength, the teeth, or the inclination."

Joseph smiled despite himself as he moved nearer. Fleetfeet took a few steps and stood next to Joseph.

"There's something very important that I must discuss with you," Steelgaze said. "A quest that must be undertaken. But I am too weak to perform the task."

"Tell us," Fleetfeet said.

"We'll do anything," Joseph added.

"I have just learned the location of an ancient map," Steelgaze said. "It is said that this map details a way through the maze of high barrier reefs that surround Dinotopia."

"Impossible!" Fleetfeet cried.

"He's right," Joseph said. "No one rolls out of the nest!"

Steelgaze nodded. "This map is a dangerous thing. I cannot say if the route it shows through the island's many dangers was ever true. But I do know this: Over the last thousand years alone, the land of Dinotopia has suffered earthquakes, floods, and hurricanes. These events have changed the island's geography.

"If someone tried to use the map now and sail from the island, it might lead to disaster. The map has to be found and destroyed at all costs. Lives are at stake!"

Joseph stepped forward, his chest swelled with pride. "I'm your man. Look no further. Just tell me where the map is and I'll go get it!"

Fleetfeet chortled. "You? By my scales! Don't you see what's happening here? *I* am to be appointed this task and *you* are here to witness the great event!"

"Boys—" Steelgaze said.

"You?" Joseph asked Fleetfeet, not hearing his mentor. "Ha! *I'm* the one who came in second at the Dinosaur Olympics!"

Fleetfeet's tail shot up in the air, then his domed head dipped to butt Joseph lightly in the chest. "You forget, Joseph, I *tied* you for second in every competition, including ring riders!"

Steelgaze shook his head.

"Besides," continued Fleetfeet, "what about that time I ran for three days to bring healing salves to the sick! I'm the best one for this job!"

"Really?" Joseph asked, planting his hands on his hips. "What about when I found the lost child during the monsoon? Hmm?"

"Boys!" Steelgaze said again, a bit louder.

"I would swim the Polongo River for an honor like this!" Fleetfeet declared. Joseph opened his mouth and was about to speak when Fleetfeet cut him off. "Against the current!"

"Boys!" Steelgaze roared.

Joseph and Fleetfeet turned sharply to look at their mentor. He seemed weaker now. His head was raised with great effort and his thick, wrinkled neck trembled. The great dinosaur's tail was still.

Joseph felt ashamed. Fleetfeet suddenly lowered his tail and turned his gaze to the floor.

"I want the two of you to take on this quest together," Steelgaze said.

Joseph's jaw dropped. Fleetfeet looked up sharply in wonder.

"The map is hidden in a secret Time Tower room . There is only one way to get inside the room."

Joseph listened attentively as Steelgaze gave detailed instructions. Then he and Fleetfeet repeated them.

"*Be careful* in telling anyone of this," Steelgaze said, and the boys nodded vigorously.

"How did you find out about it?" Joseph asked. "And why didn't someone destroy it before?"

"That doesn't matter," Steelgaze said. "All that is important is that the quest be completed and the map destroyed as soon as possible. Return to me when it's done. Now go. And *don't* send those women in after you."

Joseph and Fleetfeet bowed before their teacher. They turned and walked to the door.

"And, boys…" Steelgaze called.

The students turned. *Was this the moment?* Joseph wondered. Would Steelgaze finally say that they had truly done well, that he was proud of them? Neither had ever heard the words.

"Don't dally on the way," Steelgaze said. Then he looked up toward the window, sighing and shaking his head.

"We won't disappoint you," Joseph said. His heart was about to break from the love he felt for his teacher.

"We'll be back very soon," Fleetfeet said.

Steelgaze didn't respond. He looked as if he were falling asleep.

The boys slipped quietly from the room.

CHAPTER 3

Preparations for the journey began immediately.

"We need to go down the Polongo River," Joseph said to Townsend. "Can you help us?"

Townsend asked no questions. He made immediate arrangements for the loan of a boat.

Before midday, the boys were standing on the bow of a sleek sailboat. Constructed in the shape of a dolphin, the boat's sails rose up and unfurled like the buds of a beautiful lavender flower.

Townsend waved farewell as Joseph and Fleetfeet cast off.

"To the Time Towers!" Joseph cried.

"To adventure!" Fleetfeet responded.

The dolphin boat eased down the river, and soon Townsend was too far away to be seen.

"Do you think Steelgaze ever gave one of his students a task this important?" Joseph asked.

"Never," Fleetfeet said confidently. "If he had, we'd have heard about it."

For the first hour, the sparkling waters of the Polongo appeared to shimmer with excitement, reflecting Joseph and Fleetfeet's good mood. But as the journey went on and the sky became overcast, Joseph grew worried.

"Do you think Steelgaze will be all right?" Joseph asked. "I've never seen him so weak."

"He'll be fine," Fleetfeet said, scratching his snout. "When I was young, Steelgaze made me a promise. He said that for all my life, he would be there to guide me. And when I no longer needed him as a teacher, he would be there as a friend."

"He *said* that?" Joseph asked, amazed.

"Well…not in so many words. But it was what he meant. I'm sure of it. And I don't expect him to go back on that now."

Joseph nodded. Steelgaze was far too strong of spirit and body to leave them any time soon.

"Remember that time Steelgaze helped build the new schoolhouse?" Joseph asked. "The old house had to go, so Steelgaze used his tail. One swipe, two swipes, and down went a wall!"

Fleetfeet laughed. "And the tug of war—remember that?"

"Steelgaze on one side, twenty of us on the other, and we were the ones tugged to the mud!"

They swapped more stories about their mentor,

then they checked the sails and made a hearty lunch. There were enough provisions packed to last them a week.

As the sun came out again, they noticed the rise of the Sculpted Cliffs in the distance.

"They look like phantom mountains from here," Joseph said, admiring the beautiful azure and lavender peaks etched upon the soft blue sky. "Or the spires of a city in the clouds."

Fleetfeet rubbed his claws together. "There *are* such things, you know. Cities in the clouds."

"No, there aren't," Joseph scoffed.

The saurian leaped to his feet. "My ancestors lived in one!"

Joseph laughed. "You're just playing with me."

Fleetfeet's head darted back and forth as he looked around anxiously.

"What is it?" Joseph asked, suddenly alarmed.

"I was checking for the spirits of my ancestors," Fleetfeet said. He breathed a sigh of relief. "I don't think any of them heard you."

Joseph frowned. He knew better than to believe any of Fleetfeet's stories. And yet… "You mean you can actually see their spirits?"

"Only when they're very upset. I think we're all right for the moment. But be careful of what you say. Those who lived in the floating city are especially sensitive."

"I see." Joseph eyed his friend, wondering whether

to let him get away with his tall tale.

Oh, what the heck, thought Joseph. This stretch of the Polongo was gentle, and some entertainment would pass the time. "So, Fleetfeet, tell me about this city."

Fleetfeet's tail swung back and forth with excitement as he began. He spoke of a time long forgotten. Of beings made of clouds who told the most wonderful jokes, and of bright fiery creatures heavier than a Ceratosaurus *except* when they danced.

"...and whenever they came to the city in the clouds, they danced all the time!"

After a good hour of tales, Fleetfeet asked, "Did I tell you of the quest my great-grandfather had to undertake? To find the magical scroll that powered the great organ in our music hall?"

Joseph's eyes were wide. He'd been hanging on Fleetfeet's every word.

But the Stegoceras stretched his arms and yawned. "I'll save it for another time."

"No, tell me!"

"The story's too long, and my voice is getting tired. Another time?"

"You bet!" Joseph sat back. "Hmm."

"What is it?"

"I was just wondering. Was any of that really true?"

"Of course. And I can prove it."

"How?"

22

Fleetfeet tilted his domed head. "Why do you think we Stegoceras have such hard heads?"

"I don't know. Never really thought about it."

"It's because we were always falling from the city in the clouds and landing on them. So we *had* to evolve thicker skulls!"

"Very funny," said Joseph with a laugh. "Now try to answer this question: How did your people keep the city floating in the clouds?"

"Ah." Fleetfeet shrugged. "Hot air, of course."

"And I'm sure they had lots," said Joseph with a laugh. "After all, you've got plenty of it."

Fleetfeet dropped his head to butt his friend playfully.

"Wait, I've got one more question…"

"What?"

"Why would they want to live in a city *above* Dinotopia, anyway? Everything we could possibly want or need is here. And—"

Joseph suddenly stopped. A confused expression clouded his face. "Now that I think about it, why would anyone make a map for *leaving* the island?"

Fleetfeet thought this over before answering. "We were born on Dinotopia. So, of course, we'd never think of leaving. But there are some who might consider a map like that worth something."

"Like who?" Joseph asked.

"Dolphinbacks who are newly landed here," suggested Fleetfeet.

"That's true," said Joseph after thinking it over. "I suppose some of them left loved ones behind and might wish to see them again."

"And others might simply need time to adjust to our way of life and discover how wonderful things are here," said Fleetfeet. "They might get hurt trying to get back to the land they left behind."

"Yes," said Joseph. "I see."

"We must destroy the map to prevent such people from being taken advantage of."

"Taken advantage of?" Joseph asked. "How?"

"Someone could talk them into trading their treasured mementos for the map. And the only place that map will lead is straight to disaster."

Joseph shuddered. "I'd *never* do such a thing to a poor, trusting soul!"

"Neither would I. But I've heard there are one or two shady types who wouldn't be above making a profit that way."

"Not here," Joseph said. "Not on Dinotopia. I just can't believe it. Even Lee Crabb wouldn't do a thing like that!"

"Even so, we promised Steelgaze that we'd destroy the map. And neither of us would want to disappoint him."

"We won't. We'll find it, no matter what!"

As the sun sank in the sky, the boys tended to the sailboat and played games of Put, Take, All or Nothing and Paper, Scissors, Stone.

After a short time, Joseph grew bored. He unpacked his dragonhorn.

"Don't tell me you're going to practice now," Fleetfeet groaned.

"How else will I ever get really good?"

The saurian shook his head. He looked down at his hind claws. "What good is having fleet feet when there is nowhere I can run?"

"It's not *that* bad," Joseph said. "Listen."

He blew into his horn and a collection of blaring off-key notes emerged. Fleetfeet distracted himself by checking the sails and humming a tune.

Suddenly, a piercing cry from above made both of them fall silent and look up. A Skybax circled overhead, then dipped down toward them.

He was a magnificent creature, with a wingspan of more than a dozen yards. He had a long, graceful neck and a head almost the size of his almond-shaped torso. His wings were the colors of the most fantastic sand paintings with shades of gold and emerald, crimson, and azure. Even from this distance, Joseph could see his fierce, burning eyes.

The Skybax clearly wanted the boys' attention. He circled once more, then flew off in the direction of a small channel that branched off from the river.

"What do you think he wants?" Joseph asked.

Fleetfeet tapped Joseph's dragonhorn. "I'd say he was a music critic. And you know what? He just headed for the hills!"

Joseph raised the dragonhorn to his lips once again. "And here I thought Skybaxes had taste."

With his claw, Fleetfeet touched the horn. "They do."

Noticing movement from the corner of his eye, Joseph looked up. "The Skybax is coming back!"

"Maybe it *wasn't* your horn," Fleetfeet said.

This time, the Skybax came in low, cruising just over their masts.

"Any closer and he would have torn our sails!" Joseph cried.

"I don't think he means any harm," Fleetfeet said. "He's just desperate to get our attention. I wonder why."

"He's acting like a rolled-up scroll," Joseph muttered.

Again, the Skybax headed toward the branch of the great river. He called out and came back.

"He wants us to follow him," Fleetfeet said.

Joseph shook his head. "We can't! Steelgaze told us not to dally."

Fleetfeet's expression became grave. "But something's boiling in the pot."

"Hey, look!" Joseph said. "That Skybax doesn't have a rider, and yet he's wearing a harness."

"See, I told you. We'd better go with him."

Joseph and Fleetfeet turned their dolphin sailboat and left the Polongo River. The branch they followed quickly began to narrow. Rock walls climbed so high on either side of them that a grayness quickly descended and shadows lengthened. But the Skybax remained in sight.

Suddenly, the current changed and the water turned rough.

"What's going on?" Joseph asked.

"Something's dragging us forward." Fleetfeet kept an iron grip on the wheel. "We have to lower the sails!"

"Look!" Joseph said. He pointed at the Skybax, who had just perched on a raised area off to their left. The Skybax flapped his wings and let out a terrible cry.

"No, you look!" Fleetfeet said.

Joseph shifted his gaze. In the distance, on another cliff to their left, lay the still form of a Skybax Rider. The crimson uniform stood out among the pale shades of yellow and gray that covered the rockface.

But another object was even closer: a low stone arch that stretched from one cliff face to another.

"We have to take down the sails," Fleetfeet said. "Or they'll get snagged on the arch!"

"No, we should put in where the Skybax perched," Joseph said. "There's something wrong with the current. Even if we get past that arch—"

"We *have* to get past it or we'll have no way of reaching the rider! We have to put in closer!"

"I don't know," Joseph said.

They stared at each other.

"Paper, Scissors, Stone?" Fleetfeet suggested as a way to decide.

"All right."

The game was over quickly. Fleetfeet's choice of stone "broke" Joseph's scissors. Fleetfeet won.

The Skybax issued another shrill scream as the dolphin boat sailed past it. Joseph felt it was a warning. But his friend had made up his mind, and Fleetfeet was so stubborn!

Joseph labored to take down the sails, but the winch that lowered them was stuck.

"I can't make it budge!" Joseph hollered.

"Take the helm!" Fleetfeet commanded.

They passed one another, each nearly slipping on the slick deck. Their boat bobbed wildly in the choppy waters, and froth washed over the sides.

Straining, Fleetfeet worked the winch. Suddenly, the sails started to move. Fleetfeet laughed with relief.

As they rushed along, Joseph held the helm tightly, navigating the boat through the treacherous waters. Then Fleetfeet's laughter suddenly stopped.

They could finally see what lay beyond the archway ahead. The cliff walls ended and the channel opened into a wide lake. At its center the terrible churning waters swirled into a deadly funnel. Everything, from driftwood and leaves to trunks of trees, was being dragged into it.

They were heading right for it!

CHAPTER 4

Before the dolphin boat could be swept toward the whirlpool's point of no return, the sails caught on the archway.

A loud crash sounded as a wrenching vibration tore through the craft. The sails shattered and the boat was swept up, its bow pointing at the sky, its aft in the water.

Fleetfeet tried to grasp the fluttering sails, but his claws ripped through the material. Joseph gripped the wheel, but he could not stop the craft. Lurching to the right, it skipped like a stone until it crashed along the shore opposite the unconscious Skybax Rider.

After Fleetfeet and Joseph were flung to the sand, they looked up in time to see bits of the broken sailboat rushing into the watery funnel.

"Whoa…" Joseph whispered.

Fleetfeet looked shaken. "Are you all right?"

"Whoa…" Joseph shook his head. "I'm waiting for the world to stop spinning."

"Me too." Fleetfeet looked at the shattered boat. "We'll never get to the Time Towers now."

"We will," Joseph said. "We'll walk if we must!"

The harsh cry of the Skybax interrupted them.

Joseph rose on wobbly legs. Fleetfeet came over to help him.

"We've got to reach that rider," said Joseph.

Fleetfeet nodded. The downed Skybax Rider was on a cliff on the *other* side of the water.

"We can't swim the river," Fleetfeet said miserably. "If only I hadn't been so stubborn. We could have stopped near the Skybax, like you said. We could have found a way to reach the rider on foot, then used our oars to get back to the Polongo. But now—"

"Now we'll have to make the best of things," interrupted Joseph. He patted his friend on the back. "That's the *only* thing worth considering."

Fleetfeet nodded gratefully.

They examined the area, and Joseph soon had an idea. "It'll be difficult," he said, pointing to a nearby rise, "but if we can make the climb up there, I think we can reach the archway."

"How?"

"You'll see."

Joseph took the lead. He started to climb the rise, but his handholds gave out. He came tumbling back down, landing hard on his backside.

"So much for that idea," he grumbled.

"It was a good idea," stated Fleetfeet. "Try again!"

"No, I'll find another way."

"Wait. I want to try."

"Suit yourself."

Fleetfeet did. He climbed the rise and fell several times. But while Joseph was trying to come up with another way to reach the arch, Fleetfeet was discovering just the right path to the top. He was standing on the archway by the time Joseph noticed his progress.

"How'd you do that?" Joseph cried.

"Steelgaze taught us to never give up. Look! I made marks along the path. Climb up after me!"

Joseph happily followed in his friend's clawprints. Soon they were walking across the narrow archway. Then they scrambled up the other side of the cliff and found their way to the Skybax Rider.

The young man in the crimson tunic had straw-colored hair and a handsome face. He lay on his side, mumbling to himself between labored breaths.

"I wonder what happened?" asked Fleetfeet.

Joseph examined the rider. "I think he fell. See, around his foot? That's part of the harness. It must have broken somehow. He was lucky he landed on this ledge."

Fleetfeet nodded.

"It looks like he hurt his head," noted Joseph. "Remember what Steelgaze taught us about injuries like this?"

"Yes. We can't let him fall asleep. If he does, he might not wake up again."

A sharp cry sounded from a few hundred yards away. It was the Skybax. As if in answer, the Skybax Rider moaned. The sound captured the attention of both lads.

"Are you all right?" Fleetfeet asked the rider.

"Don't try to move," Joseph cautioned.

The rider settled onto his back. "Not much... chance of that...I feel as if I've been sat on by a Brachiosaurus. I hurt all over."

Again, the worried Skybax called out.

"I'm Rudolfo," the Skybax Rider said. "What are your names?"

"I'm Joseph. This is Fleetfeet. We were traveling down the Polongo when your Skybax got our attention and brought us here."

"It was my fault we crashed," Fleetfeet said. "Joseph wanted to put in sooner. If he had, we would have been all right. Now our boat's ruined and our quest—"

Joseph cut him off. "Our *quest* to find the best fishing this side of the Polongo will have to wait."

"Ah," Fleetfeet said. "Yes."

Joseph noticed that the Skybax Rider's eyes were beginning to shut.

"Why were you here?" Joseph asked quickly.

"I was...delivering a message."

"A message!" An idea struck Joseph. "You have a

scroll on you? A dry scroll? We could write a message on it and your Skybax can deliver it to bring more help!"

"Yes," Fleetfeet said, turning to his friend. "Then *one* of us can wait here and the other can hike back to the river to warn travelers of the whirlpool."

"Me, of course," said Joseph.

"Not you!" exclaimed Fleetfeet. "Don't you see?" With something as important as this, you only send the best. I'm sure that Steelgaze sent us both on this quest so that it would finally be made clear who is meant to lead and who to follow. And *I* know the natural order of things. After all, I led the way up here—"

"But you also made a choice that crashed the boat—" Joseph was sorry to say it, but Fleetfeet could make him so angry sometimes!

"Boys—" Rudolfo interrupted. "I have no scrolls...But you're right. We must...warn people of the...whirlpool."

"A fire is what we need," suggested Fleetfeet.

"A small fire may not be enough to get anyone's attention," Joseph pointed out

"Yes," said Rudolfo. "We need a real *blaze*—something they'll see from far off."

Joseph and Fleetfeet looked at one another. "The boat!" they said together.

"But first we need to get our supplies out," said Fleetfeet. "And besides, it won't burn all night. We'll have to wait until the Skybax brings help closer."

"I know what we need," Joseph said. "A relay, like in the Dinosaur Olympics. A dozen Skybaxes, passing the word from one to another, letting us know when to expect company."

"But we only have the one Skybax," Fleetfeet said. "By the time he arrives with help, our fire may be out."

"Brightwing—" Rudolfo began, then paused to gather strength. "His name is Brightwing, and I can hear him at distances that might surprise you."

"Then I know what we should do," Joseph said.

Fleetfeet nodded with a quick, excited jerk of his head. "As do I!"

They told Rudolfo about their new plan. He nodded his approval. Struggling, the Skybax Rider raised one hand.

There was a great screech from Brightwing, then the Skybax launched itself into the air.

Hours later, after night descended, the Skybax Rider developed a fever. Joseph mopped Rudolfo's forehead with wet rags torn from the sleeves of his shirt. But the fever grew worse.

Then, suddenly, Rudolfo turned his head and spoke. "I can hear him…"

Joseph shook his head. "I can't hear a thing. It might be the fever."

"No," insisted Rudolfo. "Please take my word for this."

Nodding, Joseph picked up his horn and started to blow. The sounds were just as disagreeable as they'd been that afternoon, but they were also just as *loud*.

Down near the river, Fleetfeet had been waiting by the wrecked sailboat. After hearing the signal, he started the fire and set their boat ablaze. It didn't take long before the entire craft was burning brightly.

Joseph put his horn down and listened. He was hoping to hear the Skybax's squalls.

But he heard nothing.

He blew the horn again, keeping watch on both the fire and the sick man next to him. After a time, the boat's flames started to ebb, but Rudolfo's fever was still climbing.

"What are we going to do?" Joseph whispered.

"Have faith," Rudolfo said. "There's nothing much any of us can do. Now play your horn again. Louder this time. As loud as you can!"

Joseph raised the horn. He blew again and again. He blew until his ribs ached. And this time, when he paused to take a breath, he heard the distant call of a Skybax!

But was the fire still bright enough to be seen? Quickly, Joseph turned to look. Yes! The flames were still alive!

A few minutes later, Brightwing appeared. He took up the perch he'd used before. Joseph saw a glow that looked like fireflies in the distance. Then he heard the shouts of people.

A boat was coming.

"Go now!" Rudolfo said. "You must help your friend warn them about the whirlpool. Go!"

Joseph quickly climbed down from the ledge. He skirted along the shoreline, blowing his horn and waving his hands frantically. Fleetfeet was suddenly behind him, waving a pair of torches.

"Stop here!" Joseph shouted. "Whirlpool ahead!"

The Skybax added its own screeching cry as Joseph and Fleetfeet ran along the shoreline. They nearly collapsed with relief when they saw that the boat's crew had heard them.

"We did it!" the boys cried together in triumph.

The boat was dropping anchor near the Skybax's perch.

CHAPTER 5

The boat had come from a nearby village. Luckily, a healer was on board.

Joseph and Fleetfeet explained the situation, and the healer went straight to the injured rider. His helpers followed, carrying bags of medicinal roots and flowers.

The two boys waited with the boat's crew for several hours. Finally, the healer came back down to shore.

"He'll be all right," the healer told them. He was a silver-bearded man with gentle green eyes. "The two of you did very well. If not for your efforts, I fear he might not have lived into the night. I wish there was a way to reward you."

"Well, what direction are you sailing?" asked Joseph hopefully. "South, perhaps?"

"No, I'm sorry. We're traveling north."

Joseph sighed heavily with disappointment.

Fleetfeet bowed his head and asked, "Could you take us back to the Polongo River, at least?"

"Of course." The healer cocked his head to one side. "Where are you going so urgently?"

Joseph didn't answer the healer. After all, he and Fleetfeet could handle this special mission for Steelgaze themselves. They didn't need any help. *And besides,* thought Joseph, *Steelgaze* had *said to* be careful *in telling anyone about the map.*

Thank goodness the Skybax Brightwing began screeching and circling overhead. It provided him with a chance to change the subject.

"He seems happy!" Joseph exclaimed.

"I think he understands that his friend will be well and that you two are responsible," the healer said. "Climb to the ledge and see if he lets you near him."

"Are you sure?" asked Joseph and Fleetfeet together.

The healer nodded, and the two did as he suggested. They reached the ledge where the Skybax had perched, then stood back as the magnificent creature landed close. Brightwing flapped his long, leathery wings several times, then bowed his head.

"I never thought I'd see such a thing!" called the healer. "He means to let you take wing!"

Joseph looked to Fleetfeet and said, "He must be mistaken. You know how skittish Skybaxes are with anyone but their riders!"

"I'm not sure," Fleetfeet said. "The way he's looking at us—it's as if he knows what's in our hearts."

From below, the healer called, "He wants to show his gratitude. Let him! The harness is repaired. There's no danger!"

Joseph swallowed uneasily. "How will he know where to take us?"

Fleetfeet walked before the Skybax. With his claw he drew a picture in the dirt to represent the Time Towers. The Skybax nodded once.

"I think that answers our question," Fleetfeet said.

After packing some light supplies in makeshift backpacks, Joseph and Fleetfeet climbed upon the Skybax. Two of the healer's assistants helped secure the inexperienced riders to the harness with a series of ropes.

"When you wish to be released, pull on this rope," one of the assistants said. "It will loosen the others."

"Thank you," Joseph said. He looked over to his friend. "I guess we're ready."

"As ready as we'll ever be," Fleetfeet said.

Brightwing let out a triumphant cry. Then the majestic creature flung himself from the cliff wall and soared out over the water.

Joseph gasped.

Fleetfeet laughed with joy!

The Skybax soared low over the waters of the canal until it reached the Polongo. Then he headed south.

Joseph didn't know how long their flight took.

The gentle flapping of the Skybax's wings was a soothing lullaby. One moment, Joseph was gazing at the stars above and the sparkling waters below. The next, he was sound asleep.

A high, sharp squawk finally woke him. He blinked several times and gasped at what he saw.

"It's so beautiful," Fleetfeet said.

Brightwing had taken them to the island of the Time Towers. The sun was rising behind the great array of spiral towers, casting them in silhouette.

"There must be hundreds of them!" Joseph said. He untied the rope holding him in place and slipped free. Fleetfeet did the same. Brightwing unfurled his great wings, shaking off the last of the ropes. With a final cry, the Skybax took to the air again.

Joseph and Fleetfeet waved good-bye to Brightwing, then they turned to face the towers.

"You missed a lot by falling asleep on the journey," Fleetfeet said.

"I was tired." Joseph stretched. "What happened?"

"For one thing, Brightwing took us high into the sky."

"He did?"

"Yes. We soared through the clouds. And we danced and sang with the spirits of my people."

Joseph frowned. "The ones who lived in a city supported by hot air?"

"The very same."

"Well, you should wake me up next time. It's about time you introduced me to them."

"I tried," Fleetfeet said. "But your shell is thicker than mine, and there was just no way to get your attention."

Joseph shrugged. "Too late to worry about it now. We've got something more important to think about, anyway."

Fleetfeet nodded. The boys studied the scene before them. Directly ahead lay a fantastic city populated by the many timepieces that had been used on Dinotopia.

These structures were retired from use now, except to stand as monuments to the gradual passing of time they'd once measured for Dinotopians throughout the centuries.

As Joseph and Fleetfeet approached the outskirts of the time village, they noticed that many of the towers were covered with strange writing.

"What language is that?" Joseph asked.

"I haven't a clue," Fleetfeet said. "An ancient tongue, I would guess."

The maze of timepieces was a fascinating place. The two boys studied each twisting spiral structure. Some were no taller than an average man. Others were as great as a Brachiosaurus.

Some were made of stone, others carved from wood, and still others fashioned from metal. A few were even made of gold. And one very tall tower was chiseled out of crystal.

As the sun slowly rose in the sky, elegant patterns began to appear on the towers.

41

"Look," Fleetfeet said. "There are crystal beacons at the top of many of the towers."

Joseph pointed at the tall crystal tower. In the bright morning sunlight, the tower was almost blinding to look at. Shafts of brilliance stretched outward and touched the crystals atop the other towers. The light was bounced from one tower to another, creating patterns above.

"The patterns form words," Joseph said. "The beams of light are writing messages!"

"You're right," Fleetfeet said, reading the words out loud. "*All the time—in the world—*"

"*—is here,*" finished Joseph in awe. He'd witnessed many strange and glorious sights growing up on Dinotopia, but nothing like this.

The boys blinked and looked at each other. Sounds were rising around them. A soft, beautiful trilling seemed to come from everywhere—and nowhere—all at once.

They sensed movement around them, too. Suddenly, dozens of small saurians, Harpymimuses, appeared from behind the towers. They barely noticed the two travelers who had come so far to stand among the beautiful spires.

"They're singing," Joseph whispered.

"It's beautiful," Fleetfeet said. "Though I don't know the song."

The saurians moved quickly along the outer ridges of the timepieces, silk cloths in their claws. They began to polish the towers with great care.

"Hold on," Joseph said. "According to Steelgaze's instructions, we need to climb three of these towers, just as they're doing. How are we going to do that if our friends here are in the way?"

"Don't put the cart before the Brachiosaurus. First, we have to *find* the three towers. They're supposed to be located around the great timepiece known as Sun Li's Folly."

"Yes," said Joseph, "and remember Steelgaze said that not every timepiece here is of Dinotopian design. Sun Li's Folly was one such timepiece, so we'll have to look sharp."

As the boys walked deeper into the maze of spiral towers, they began to notice some very odd timepieces that had been built by people who'd come from other lands. There was a tall box with a face and a pendulum.

"That's a grandfather clock," said Joseph. "I know a newcomer who built one for his new home on Dinotopia."

"What's that?" asked Fleetfeet, stopping before another timepiece.

Both boys jumped at once as a tiny bird suddenly leaped out of a door and squawked at them. "Cuckoo! Cuckoo! Cuckoo!"

"What does 'cuckoo' mean, anyway?" asked Fleetfeet after the two stopped laughing.

"Beats me," said Joseph. "C'mon. Let's keep moving."

They continued to pass more monuments to time.

They continued to pass more monuments to time. One was a primitive timekeeper—a simple stick that cast a shadow. Then came a pair of odd sundials, a beautiful hourglass, and a water clock. Mechanical clocks and more of those with pendulums soon followed.

"Still no sign of Sun Li's Folly." Joseph sighed.

"It's got to be here...do you know anything about it?"

"Yes," said Joseph. "My mother once told me the story of how it was built. Haven't I told you?"

"It's been a long time since I've heard it," said Fleetfeet. "Why don't you tell it again?"

CHAPTER 6

"Sun Li was a man from a far-off land," said Joseph as they moved through the city of timepieces, "and from the moment the dolphins guided him safely to our shore, this newcomer thought only of time. Time lost, time saved, time going by in seconds, minutes, hours…"

"Yes," said Fleetfeet. "And according to the Dinotopian philosophy, *time marches on, but history repeats itself.*"

"Right," said Joseph. "The timekeeper explained this belief to Sun Li, but the man didn't agree with it. He said that if time was properly understood, then there would be no need for history to repeat itself."

Fleetfeet nodded. "I see. So Sun Li confused what he was told with the old saying that those who do not learn from history are doomed to repeat it."

"Yes—which is wrong," pointed out Joseph. "That saying has nothing to do with our teachings. When we say that history repeats itself, we mean that all life is a *cycle*. That one must be in tune with the rhythm of life and our planet."

"Right," agreed Fleetfeet. "Inner harmony comes from knowing when to plant crops, when to tend to the young, when to fix dams, and when to allow hatchlings to leave the nest."

As Fleetfeet spoke, Joseph noticed one of the small Harpymimuses waving a happy hello from atop a spiral Time Tower. Joseph waved back, and the little saurian put his head down again, going back to his important work.

"Sun Li saw time as his enemy," said Joseph, finishing up the story. "He longed to be freed from what he saw as its restraints. He didn't understand that these bonds existed only within his imagination. And so he built a clock."

"A mighty clock," Fleetfeet added.

"An *enormous* clock, housed within a forty-foot tower. In fact," Joseph said, "I see it right now!"

The lads had arrived. Sun Li's Folly stood before them. The tower had a movable roof that was now closed. Chinese symbols covered the many brown and black panels on the tower walls.

"We have to get inside," Joseph said.

Fleetfeet turned. "I see them now. Three smaller Time Towers, each the same distance from Sun Li's

Folly—and from one another. Just like Steelgaze told us."

"And none of them are being cleaned. We're in luck. All that remains is for us to decide who will have the honor of activating the mechanism."

"I thought we had resolved that," Fleetfeet said. "The honor goes to the fastest!"

The Stegoceras dropped his backpack and instantly bolted toward one of the towers.

Yelping in surprise, Joseph dropped his pack, too, then raced to the tower opposite. He flew up the steps that ran along the outside of the structure, slowing only a little as he climbed to a dangerous height.

There were no crystal beacons in these towers. Instead, there was a special box with ten wooden squares, "buttons" that had to be pressed in a particular order.

"First three push, second three skip, next two push, last two skip!" repeated Joseph to himself, recalling Steelgaze's instructions. Then the Kentrosaurus had added, *Sixty seconds is the time you have on all three towers. Measure it out evenly...*

Joseph followed the "combination" as the first step to opening the lock. He quickly pressed the required square blocks, leaving the others untouched.

"That didn't take anywhere near sixty seconds," Joseph mumbled to himself, a bit puzzled. But the combination *did* seem to be working. When he'd pressed the last square, he heard a loud click echo throughout the tower.

"Ha!" came a voice from the ground.

Joseph looked down to see Fleetfeet running for the third tower.

"Best two out of three!" Fleetfeet called.

Joseph scrambled down from his tower. But by the time he reached the third tower, Fleetfeet was already halfway up the spiral. Joseph knew that he'd been defeated, and so he waited to hear his friend shout his victory.

"I did it!" Fleetfeet cried.

Sighing, Joseph turned to Sun Li's Folly. The roof would open at any moment now. Then they could climb the tower, enter through the roof, and climb down to find the hidden room within. That's where the map would be sitting.

But nothing happened.

"I don't understand!" Fleetfeet called. "The roof is not moving. What went wrong?"

Joseph didn't know—and decided that now was not the time to find out. He'd been given a second chance and he wasn't about to squander it!

Racing to the top of the closest spire, Joseph pressed the required square blocks. The mechanism clicked, beginning to engage.

As he came down along the spiral, he saw Fleetfeet racing for another tower. He reached the top as Joseph got to the base of the third tower. Now it would be *his* turn to crow in triumph!

But when Joseph pressed the combination of

blocks in this tower, he met with the same sorry result that Fleetfeet had. The blocks descended, but there was no "click." The depressed squares simply rose up again, resetting themselves. The roof on Sun Li's Folly hadn't budged.

Frustrated, Joseph climbed down from the tower. He saw Fleetfeet barreling toward him, his domed head down in a butting position to warn Joseph to move out of the way.

Joseph had no desire to feel the bump of Fleetfeet's hard head, so he stepped quickly aside. As Fleetfeet barreled by, Joseph found a shady spot to sit down and think.

Why aren't Steelgaze's instructions working? Joseph asked himself.

After watching Fleetfeet race from one tower to the other more than a dozen times, the answer came to him. This was not a task that could be done *alone*. That's why Steelgaze had sent them both!

"Claw-brother," Joseph called. "I have an idea."

"No, I almost have it!" Fleetfeet cried breathlessly, his legs wobbling beneath him.

But Joseph stopped him. "Do you remember when Steelgaze told us 'Sixty seconds is the count for all three towers. Measure it out evenly'?"

"Yes," said Fleetfeet, his breathing still labored.

"Don't you see? We don't have sixty seconds for *each* tower. We have sixty for them *all*. And if we 'measure it out evenly,' then that means we must depress each set of square blocks twenty seconds apart."

Fleetfeet considered this a moment. "But if we did it that way, which of us would be the winner?"

"If we find the map? Both of us."

The saurian agreed. He climbed one of the three towers and waited.

"Now, if this doesn't work," Joseph called up to him, "we'll wait until you're rested and you can be the one doing the running."

"I am faster, of course," Fleetfeet said. "You've never beaten me in a foot race."

"I've never really tried," Joseph said, who always knew there was no point in trying to defeat a saurian called Fleetfeet in a foot race. "Are you ready?"

"Yes."

"Count to twenty after I give the signal, then engage the mechanism."

"It won't work," Fleetfeet predicted. "We should just try to run faster."

"If it doesn't work, we'll go back to your plan," answered Joseph.

"All right."

Joseph climbed up to the small platform at the top of the second tower. He took his time, not wishing to exhaust himself. When he was ready, he pressed the proper blocks, then shouted, "I'm going!"

Next he turned and ran down the spiral's steps. As he passed Fleetfeet's tower, he heard the saurian counting. "...eighteen, nineteen, twenty. I'm pressing the blocks!" Fleetfeet cried.

The third and final tower beckoned. Counting to himself, Joseph raced to the top and engaged the mechanism.

This time, the blocks did not reset themselves as they had on all the other attempts. Joseph heard a massive click through the tower where he stood, then he felt a rumbling beneath him, a trembling that seemed to reach into the very ground!

A loud roar sounded from Sun Li's Folly. Joseph turned to see the wooden roof split noisily, each half sliding back.

The lock had worked! It simply took *two* people, working together, to coordinate the timing of opening the mechanism.

"We did it!" Joseph cried.

Fleetfeet howled and whooped with delight. Both boys scrambled down from their spiral towers and raced to the wooden edifice.

Climbing up the side was no problem. There was a ladder for just such a purpose. Soon they stood on the roof, looking down at the top of a dome. All manner of gears, pulleys, and strange mechanisms sparkled in the warm sunlight.

Joseph spotted a series of rungs leading down into the central chamber of the vast timepiece. They climbed down and started looking around for the secret chamber.

In an alcove filled with spare parts, they spotted the symbol Steelgaze had told them about. "There it is!" they called out together.

The symbol was a carving of a human and a saurian, hand and claw joined in friendship.

"But there's another one over here," Fleetfeet said, pointing at the wall, six feet to one side of the symbol.

"And one here, too," Joseph said, spotting a third symbol on the wall, six feet to the other side of the first one.

Joseph touched the symbol in the middle. Nothing happened. They tried each symbol, but the results were the same.

"I think we need to touch all three of them at once," Fleetfeet said. "But there are just two of us."

"Try using your tail," Joseph said. "Tail for one symbol, claw for another."

Fleetfeet nodded excitedly. His tail just reached the far symbol, his claw the center one. Joseph touched the last one.

A rumbling came, and a door sank backward, revealing a darkened chamber.

"What's that bad smell?" Joseph asked.

"Age, I suppose," Fleetfeet said. "Let me go first, since I can see better in the dark." He climbed over a pile of gears and entered the room. Joseph was right behind him.

"It's empty," Fleetfeet said. "Steelgaze said the map would be in a gold-colored box lying on the floor in the center of the room. But it's not here!"

Joseph's eyes were adjusting to the darkness. In the dust, he could see a long rectangle where the box had obviously once sat. Footprints were all around it. Footprints the boys had not made.

"Someone else was here first!" cried Fleetfeet.

"Look, I've found something," Joseph said, snatching up a cloth from the floor.

"I've found something, too," Fleetfeet said. "I think it's what was giving off that bad smell."

They left the chamber so that they could examine what they'd found in the light.

"It's a handkerchief," Joseph said, staring at the cloth. "Look at that insignia in the corner."

"The Black Fish Tavern has something like that over its door, I've been told." Fleetfeet opened his claw to display the stubby prize he'd found. "A cigar."

"Who do we know who smokes cigars and goes to the Black Fish Tavern?" Joseph asked.

Fleetfeet sighed wearily. "Lee Crabb."

"And he's got the map," Joseph whispered. "We've got to get it back."

"He can't be working alone," Fleetfeet said. "Look what it took for the two of us to get into this place."

"I agree," Joseph said.

"So where do we start looking for him?"

Joseph held up the handkerchief from the Black Fish Tavern. "Where, indeed..."

CHAPTER 7

The Black Fish Tavern was a long way off, and Joseph and Fleetfeet were without a boat.

"There must be boats of some kind here at the Time Towers," Joseph said encouragingly.

"Let's talk to the little fellows who tend the time-pieces," Fleetfeet suggested.

They found a group of the small saurians heading to polish the towers on which Joseph and Fleetfeet had just been racing.

Not one of the dinosaurs was more than three feet from head to tail. They had small heads, wide eyes, and long necks. Their bodies were brown on top, with golden underbellies. If they stepped into the brush, they would blend in perfectly.

A few of them waved happily as they went on with their work.

"I'm Fleetfeet, and this is Joseph," the Stegoceras said, approaching them.

"We need your help," Joseph added. "Our boat was destroyed and we need to find a way downriver."

One of the Harpymimuses sang, "People come, people go. They bring their boats, they take their boats."

"Are there any boats left behind?" Fleetfeet asked.

"There are some, there are none," the saurian sang happily. "Time is fleeting, but there is always time."

"If we find a craft, may we borrow it?" Joseph asked.

"What is ours, what is yours? So very different, so very much the same."

Joseph looked to his friend. "I think that was a yes."

"So do I," Fleetfeet said. "We thank you!"

"As you were before, as you will be again," the saurian said.

"Yes," Joseph said, wondering what on earth the Harpymimus was talking about. "Whatever you say!"

They searched the coastline of the Time Towers island and found the harbor. A few small crafts were tied up there. Nothing so fancy as the dolphin sailboat they had crashed, but one was large enough to get them downriver.

Inside the vessel, they secured their backpacks, which were full of supplies they'd scavenged from the dolphin boat. Then the boys untied their craft and set off.

The day wore on as they sailed along.

"So what do we do with Lee Crabb when we find him?" Joseph asked.

"We convince him to give us the map. He probably doesn't realize how dangerous it could be. But we'll make sure he knows."

"What if he still won't give it to us?" Joseph asked. "I've heard he's an ornery sort."

"We'll do everything we can to honor our promise to Steelgaze," Fleetfeet said. "And it does seem that when we put our hard heads together, there's not much we can't do."

"I agree with that, claw-brother," Joseph said, putting his hand on his friend's shoulder.

The sun was at its zenith when Joseph spoke up. "At that last bend I saw the Black Fish not far downriver. Let's pull the boat onto shore and hide it in the brush. We can walk the rest of the way to the tavern."

"Good idea," said Fleetfeet. "After all, there's no telling what we'll meet up with. Better to keep the boat safe here."

Both boys were ready for a nice walk, anyway. The borrowed boat had been a great help, but it was very small and cramped. Stretching their legs sounded wonderful at this moment.

But before they turned the boat in, the boys saw something floating on the horizon. At first they couldn't quite see what it was. But, as they neared, they saw one large shape drifting through the waters while three smaller forms darted around it.

The boys weren't frightened. But they were curious. A few moments later, they finally had a good look at what was ahead.

"A dolphinback," Joseph whispered.

"With an escort," Fleetfeet noted.

The dolphinback was a girl with short black hair. She was tied to a large chunk of wood that might once have been a part of a ship. A trio of dolphins guarded her, nudging her along toward the shore.

"We have to help," Joseph said.

"It's that or let the dolphins try to untie those knots," Fleetfeet said. "And I don't think they'd have an easy time of it."

The dolphins saw them now. They leaped with joy in and out of the water. The girl on the makeshift raft never raised her head, but she moved slightly, her hand seeming to reach outward.

Joseph and Fleetfeet guided their boat to the shore, and the dolphins eased their precious guest toward them.

Joseph jumped into the water and swam toward the dolphins and their prize. He helped guide the girl in toward shore as the dolphins swam away, chirping with happiness.

Turning, Joseph saw that Fleetfeet was pulling their boat onto shore. Soon, the girl was safely on the beach, as well. Fleetfeet used his sharp claws to sever the bonds holding her to the large slab of wood. Joseph pulled her loose and set her down on her back upon the sands. She wore a long dressing gown that was soaked through.

"Stay with her," Fleetfeet said. "I'll get her something to drink."

Joseph nodded. He watched Fleetfeet disappear into the jungle, then heard a soft moan from the dolphinback. Her eyes were flickering open and her hands went out before her, as if she was reaching for something.

"Father!" she called.

Joseph felt a sudden weight descend upon his heart. The young woman looked up at him.

"Who might you be?" she whispered hoarsely.

"Don't try to talk. My friend has gone to find something to soothe your throat. He'll be back in a moment."

"My father," she croaked, rising to her feet.

Joseph shook his head. "You were alone. I'm sorry."

"He's gone then. Father's really gone." She was quiet a long moment. Then her eyes looked up into Joseph's concerned face. "I'm Teegan," she whispered.

"Joseph."

Teegan turned her gaze back to the water and watched the dolphins playing in the distance. "They saved me," she said, her voice raw. "I know that must sound crazy, but—"

"Joseph, I've found some coconuts! See!"

Joseph and Teegan turned to see Fleetfeet approaching.

58

Teegan's face drained of color. Shuddering, she backed away, edging toward the water.

Fleetfeet stopped. "Was it something I said? You don't like coconuts?"

He cracked one of them open with his claws and held it out to her.

"It speaks," she whispered. "It's Bedlam for me. The *lizard* speaks!"

CHAPTER 8

"I'm no lizard," Fleetfeet said in a voice that sounded strange and squawky to Teegan. "I'm a Stegoceras."

"What did it say?" she asked Joseph. "The words almost sound familiar, but..."

Joseph took the coconut from Fleetfeet and drank some of its milk, then he held it out. "Here, drink from this. It's good."

She nodded, reaching up for the cracked shell in his hands.

"Fleetfeet, open another one," said Joseph.

Teegan's gaze shot back to the saurian. He cracked open another coconut and stepped closer. With trembling hands, she took it from him. Her finger brushed his claws. "You're warm!"

"What'd you expect?" asked Fleetfeet. "There's no chill in the air. Just a nice breeze."

Teegan eyed the dinosaur warily, then looked to Joseph. "What did it say?"

"Not *it*," said Joseph. "*He.* This is Fleetfeet. You may find the saurian way of speaking difficult to understand at first. Just listen closely, and you'll catch on. Fleetfeet asked you what you expected."

"I—I—" She sighed. "I don't know." She sipped some of the coconut milk. "That's so good." Then she stared at Fleetfeet again. "Is this really happening?"

"To the best of my knowledge," Fleetfeet said.

Teegan blinked, as if she'd understood him better this time. "Are you sure I'm not still floating on the waves...seeing things?"

"Would it make you feel better if I said you were?" asked Fleetfeet.

"No."

"Well, you're not."

Teegan thought of her beloved father, a scholar and professor back in Scotland. She wondered what he would want her to do. The reality of his loss nearly tore her heart to pieces, though she'd known for some time that it was coming. He'd been very sick.

They had talked many times about how life would be for Teegan after he was gone, and he'd always said the same thing to her: *Whatever you do, promise me with your heart that you won't be wastin' your Heaven-given time on grief over me, fair girl. I want you to live your life well. Seek your dreams, and seek adventures. They're before you now, they are. Don't let 'em get away! And that's how you'll best remember me!*

Teegan recalled her father's words—and wishes.

She closed her eyes a moment, telling him silently that she'd at least try to live up to them. When she opened her eyes again, she found herself staring at Fleetfeet.

"What *are* you?" she asked without thinking.

The Stegoceras opened his mouth to speak.

"Are there others like you?" Teegan suddenly continued, her questions pouring out now. "What is this place? This can't be China. I know China's supposed to be odd, but not this odd—"

"Well, you see—" Joseph began.

"—and those trees," she said, pointing. "This looks like a tropical island. But the plants are like nothing I've ever seen in a book. Mind you, books have been my life up to now, so if there were things like this in books, I'd have seen them."

An odd expression came over her lovely, yet still-pale features. She took another sip of coconut milk, then set down the shell. *This is a marvelous place*, Teegan thought. *You'd have loved it here, Father. But you are* here, *aren't you? In my heart...*

By heavens, I'll live the adventure for the both of us, I will!

Teegan struggled to her feet. She didn't object when Fleetfeet took her arm and helped her.

"Tee-hee," she giggled, her spirit lighter.

"What?" Fleetfeet asked, trying not to become annoyed at the dolphinback's odd behavior.

"I had a pet lizard once," Teegan said, feeling quite giddy. *I'm Alice gone down the rabbit hole*, she thought.

She'd read the book *Alice in Wonderland* just before their ship had departed. Where she'd come from, it was quite the new sensation!

"A pet!" Fleetfeet cried.

"Aye. But not as big as you!"

"I am *not* a lizard."

"It was a salamander. We named her Lilabell. After a character in a pirate novel. A swashbuckling adventure."

"Well," Fleetfeet said, "you did get the swashbuckling part right."

"I'll swash *your* buckle," Joseph complained to his friend as he took Teegan's other arm. As she swung around to look at him, he quickly fixed a smile on his face. "Now, what was it you wanted to see?" he asked her.

"Those leaves," Teegan said. "Up ahead."

They took Teegan closer to the jungle ahead. She took her time, examining the exotic flora. "Magnolias. Ginkgoes. I *have* seen these in books. Just not this large." She turned to Fleetfeet. "And now I understand what you are."

"I told you, I'm a Stegoceras," Fleetfeet said.

"You're what Sir Richard Owen called *Dinosauria.* That's right. That's what you are. And don't try to deny it."

"All right, you've got me," Fleetfeet said.

Teegan straightened up. "It all makes sense if you stop to think about it—an uncharted island in the middle of nowhere. How did your ancestors survive here for all these years?"

"We went underground," Fleetfeet said, impressed at how quickly Teegan was catching on. "During the cold time, we developed our society underground. Then later we moved to the surface."

"You wear clothes and you speak very well," she continued. "So you're civilized, if not always civil. Is that right?"

"I'm *civil!*" Fleetfeet cried.

"Of course you are," Teegan said with a laugh. "I'm just having a go at you. A sense of humor—good to know you have one." Then Teegan sighed. "Considering you and Joseph here appear to be friends, I'd say it's safe to assume that you're peaceful, and not a meat-eater."

"Goodness, no!" Fleetfeet said.

"Well, I am," Teegan said.

Fleetfeet held back a cry of unease.

"But I suppose I'll have to adjust." A look of sadness came into her eyes. "Just as I'll have to adjust to life without my father. He was very sick, you see. His dream was to travel to foreign lands while he still could. To have as much adventure before…well…" She shook her head. "Now I'll just have to have *twice* the adventure—for him as well as me."

Joseph and Fleetfeet regarded one another. Any fears they'd had over Teegan's ability to adapt to this strange new land had been squarely set to rest.

"Now," Teegan said. "What other kinds of Dinosauria exist on this dinosaur utopia of yours?"

Joseph was about to speak.

"All of them, I would guess," Teegan said, cutting him off. She turned to Fleetfeet. "And are they all as kind and chivalrous as you?"

"Sadly, no," Fleetfeet said. "I am one of a kind."

"But there are other kinds of Dinosauria?"

"Many! You're right about that. Bravo, dear lady." Fleetfeet bowed slightly.

"You're one of a kind, all right," Joseph said.

"And you!" Teegan said. "Are all the young men as handsome, strong, and gentle as you?"

Joseph grinned. "Not a chance. I'm it. Truly."

Teegan laughed. "Now you're both having me on. And I'm enjoying every minute of it!"

Fleetfeet touched Teegan's arm, making her giggle once more. "Would you excuse us for a moment?"

"Of course, my brave and errant knights," she said, then turned to examine more flora.

Fleetfeet led Joseph a few steps into the jungle for some privacy.

"She called *me* her 'brave and errant knight,'" Joseph said with a grin.

"That's what she called us *both*. Don't let it go to your head. Especially considering neither of us is so sure what it means."

"Can't have everything," Joseph said.

"Listen. We're on a quest for Steelgaze. A hazardous map has been stolen and we have to get it back. We can't do that *and* take care of Teegan at the same time."

"I know. Someone's going to have to take her to Waterfall City so she can be taken care of. Look, she obviously needs clothes, shelter. And she'll need to begin learning our ways—"

"I have a feeling she's going to be teaching *us* about our ways before long," said Fleetfeet. "But you're right. She must be taken to Waterfall City. How about this: We're going to the Black Fish Tavern. We'll find someone there to take her."

"No, no, no," said Joseph, shaking his head. "That's no good at all."

"Why not? I know the Black Fish Tavern doesn't have the best reputation, but I'm sure we'll find *some* decent fellows there who'll agree to do the right thing."

"Sure," Joseph said. "If we tell them about the map. Which we can't. Otherwise, they'll just ask us why we're not doing it. No, I think *you* should be the one to take her."

"Me!" exclaimed Fleetfeet, his domed head dropping a bit and butting at Joseph's shoulder. "But it was *your* idea!"

"Right," said Joseph, nudging his friend away. "So *I've* done the hard part already—thinking up the plan. The least you can do is be a pal and take her back on the boat we borrowed. As it is, I'll have to find some other means of transport. This won't be easy on me."

"I see," Fleetfeet said. "And I don't suppose this has anything to do with what I said before about my being Steelgaze's *obvious* choice for this quest. That *I* was to lead and you were to follow."

"Perish the thought."

"I wish it would," argued Fleetfeet. "But the truth is, I could walk right into the Black Fish Tavern and learn all there is to know about Lee Crabb in five minutes flat."

"I could do it in half that time!" boasted Joseph. "And while you're taking Teegan to Waterfall City, I will."

"She's not comfortable with saurians yet. You should take her."

"But you can have the honor of acting as the ambassador for saurians across the island," said Joseph. "I'm sure by the time you get back to Waterfall City—"

A rustling came from above. Both lads looked up to see Teegan climbing across the branch of a tall tree. She was looking down at them.

"And what might be so special about this map?" she asked with a grin.

Joseph and Fleetfeet both sighed. A feeling of guilt rippled through them. How much had Teegan heard? Had they hurt her feelings? That's the last thing they wanted to do. It was just that their mission was so important!

"It seems to me," Teegan said as she climbed down to them, "that neither of you would have the first idea how to get along without the other. That in mind, I can't imagine why you'd both be trying so hard to continue with this mysterious quest of yours on your own."

"It's not that," Joseph said.

"Oh?" she chirped as she dropped to the ground, crossing her arms over her chest. "Faith! Each of you made quite the show of trying to get rid of the other."

Joseph felt ashamed. "I'm sorry. You must not think much of your 'errant knights' now."

"Just the opposite," Teegan said. "The truth is, I felt a little frightened of you two, and of this place. I always talk up a storm when I'm nervous, I do. But now—well, a friend of mine has brothers. I can see now that you're much like them—sharing such rivalries! And if a pair like that can exist here, too, then Dinotopia isn't so unlike where I came from after all. It's a comfort, it is Aye, one I appreciate."

Joseph opened his mouth to speak, but Teegan wasn't finished yet. "And to show you how much I appreciate it, I'll be happy to *join* you on your quest."

Joseph's shoulders sagged in defeat at the exact same time as Fleetfeet's.

"So," Teegan said, taking an arm of each errant knight, "do you want to tell me about it? Or should I figure the whole thing out as we go along? It may take me as much as ten minutes, the way I catch on to

68

things. All of us MacGregors are gifted that way. Did I mention that?"

"I thought you only went 'on and on' when you were nervous," Fleetfeet groused.

"Or when I'm excited," Teegan said. "Or very tired. Or…"

Teegan continued—on and on—as the three of them headed along the shoreline.

Soon they could hear the sound of laughter. The Black Fish Tavern was near.

CHAPTER 9

"It's like something out of one of my picture books!" Teegan cried as she got her first look at the Black Fish Tavern. "I don't think I've ever seen anything so splendid in all my life!"

Joseph hesitated. What he saw was a rather dark building with a scaly roof, a strange crystal in one spire, and the faces of fierce sea creatures peering out from every corner.

The tavern was located on the shore of the river, near an outlet that led right to the sea. The dock it stood on was wet and slippery. Boards were broken and sometimes missing. Strange submersibles, used for scouring the sea floor for sunken treasure, bobbed in the water nearby. And strong but shifty-looking characters wandered in and out of the place.

Some of the clientele were men wearing brightly colored clothing and carrying drinking vessels made from shells. Others were dinosaurs with fierce armor. They glared at the newcomers, though one seemed wobbly enough to tip off his clawed feet at any second.

Soft golden light drifted outward from the tavern and the sounds of revelry echoed from within.

"Just splendid," Teegan repeated.

"We *are* talking about the same place, aren't we?" Joseph asked.

"Indeed we are!" Fleetfeet said, taking Teegan's arm *and* the lead. He pointed to his many-colored vest. "And I believe at least *one* of us is dressed for the occasion."

They walked past a collection of scurvy knaves, doing their best to ignore the strange looks they received, and went inside. The taproom was brightly lit. A dozen humans and saurians sat at tables. A man with arms practically the size of Joseph's chest gripped the claw of a Camptosaurus, his forehead bright red from the effort of arm-wrestling.

A pair of Thescelosauruses swung from the chandelier, whooping and hollering. A dark-haired woman wearing a flaming red skirt and a white blouse delivered ale to customers while a Parksosaurus watched warily from behind a long wooden bar.

A collection of flasks and glasses hung from a shelf and paintings of humans and saurians were crammed on the wall behind. Music came from a pair of Dromiceiomimuses who played a harpsichord with both their claws and their tails.

"By my claws, what have we here?" the Parksosaurus tavern-keeper said.

At his words, all noise and activity came to an abrupt halt.

Almost all.

The human and saurian who'd been arm-wrestling were still sweating and grunting. A Dryptosaurus absently reached out a single claw and ended the contest, pinning both hand and claw to the table.

"Eh?" the two cried in unison. The moment they saw the trio, they also fell silent.

"This might not have been the best idea we ever had," Joseph whispered.

"Let me handle this," Teegan said, breaking from the arms of her companions.

"You!" Fleetfeet squawked. "But—"

"Listen up, ye bunch o' miscreants, hooligans, and ne'er-do-wells!" Teegan shouted.

The saurian who'd been arm-wrestling tilted his head. "I say, I do believe she was being just a touch redundant."

"Merciful me," added the huge man who'd been his wrestling partner.

Teegan swaggered forward. "Call me Anne Bonny!" she said. "This here's me mate, Calico Jack, and his friend, Edward Teach!"

"Ah!" said the barman. "The Stegoceras would be our old mate Jack because of his vest, wouldn't that be so?"

"It would indeed," Teegan said.

Behind her, Joseph and Fleetfeet exchanged mortified glances.

"Everyone!" the tavern-keeper said. "We have before us a bit of living history. I present to you the nefarious marauders of the deep, the woman pirate Anne Bonny and her pirate friends Calico Jack and Blackbeard!"

Every gaze in the place drifted to Joseph's clean-shaven face.

His hand instinctively brushed his smooth cheek. "Um—I'm going for a new look?"

The residents of the Black Fish Tavern erupted in laughter. The music and all the rest of the commotion quickly picked up again. Another saurian slipped behind the bar and busied himself with filling a number of drinking vessels.

"Now, what can I do for you?" the tavern-keeper said as Teegan and her friends approached.

"For starters, you can tell me who I'm talking to!" Teegan declared.

"Ah," said the tavern-keeper. "Of course. How rude of me." He put one claw to his chest. "I'm Skull." He gestured at his companion. "And this is Duggery."

Teegan laughed. "No, what are your *real* names?"

The saurian just looked at her. "I'm Skull. This is Duggery."

"Oh," she whispered. "Well, actually, I'm Teegan

MacGregor of the Clan MacGregor, and these are my friends, Joseph and Fleetfeet."

"Well," Skull said, "a bit of advice, if you're open to it."

"Of course," Teegan said, smiling, confident, and startlingly radiant in the rich golden light.

Joseph stared at her, amazed at the transformation. "Well," Joseph whispered to Fleetfeet, "she did say she learned most of what she knows about life from books, didn't she?"

"Hush," Fleetfeet replied. "I want to hear this."

"Next time, at least get the lad an eye-patch," Skull said.

"I'd say," Duggery chirped in. "He looks too wholesome to be a proper pirate. Let alone a knave who liked to line the brim of his hat with burning fuses and make people walk the plank."

"Humph!" Joseph frowned and crossed his arms under his chest.

Fleetfeet's body trembled with waves of laughter.

"What are you laughing about, Lilabell?" snapped Joseph.

Fleetfeet straightened up and cleared his throat. "We're here on most urgent business."

"Ah, I can see that," Skull said.

Teegan winked. "Can you tell us where we might find an old friend of ours?"

"And who might that be?" asked Skull.

"Lee Crabb."

"Friends of old Lee, are you!" Skull roared as he planted both claws loudly on the bar before him. Teegan, Joseph, and Fleetfeet all took a step back. All eyes were once again on them and the tavern again fell silent.

"Now," Skull said. "Are you sure you didn't read about *him* in a book somewhere?"

"Oops," Joseph whispered. He'd forgotten what good hearing Parksosauruses possessed.

"Find out what they want with old Lee!" an old white-haired man said, raising his cane.

"Aye!" cried an Arrhinoceratops. "We of the Black Fish Tavern take care of our own!"

Joseph stepped forward. With the stark importance of Steelgaze's mission on his mind, he leveled his most fearsome stare at the tavern-keeper. "Lee Crabb took something that is mine. And I mean to have it back."

There was no trace of Joseph's apparent youth in either his tone or his delivery. This was a man, not a boy, who stood firm and made the statement.

One of the saurians in the back of the tavern called, "Lee's up to his usual mischief!"

"Then all's well!" another called.

And the merriment began again.

Skull said, "This sounds like a serious business. Hmm. Where to find Lee Crabb? Well, he's not here, obviously. It's a head-scratcher, I'm afraid."

"So you don't know where he is?" Fleetfeet asked.

"That's not what I said." Skull shrugged. "Information comes at a price. Nothing's cheap around here."

"We have no gold," Joseph said. "Is there a barter we could arrange?"

"Perhaps," Skull said. "Things have been a bit dull around here lately. We need some excitement to liven things up. I think a few good old-fashioned contests would do the trick!"

"What kind of contests?" Teegan asked.

"Well, now! If I tell you *that* before you agree to things, then the whole deal will be far less interesting, don't you think?"

CHAPTER 10

Joseph looked to his friend. Fleetfeet nodded. "Agreed. But leave the dolphinback out of it," said Joseph.

"Who?" Teegan asked.

The serving maid walked by Teegan. "That's you," she whispered. Then she studied the girl's filthy, soggy clothes and said, "Come with me, Mistress Bonny. I'll get you some proper clothes!"

Soon Joseph and Fleetfeet were taken to the rear of the Black Fish, where a rickety dock stretched out over a pond filled with brackish water. Dozens of onlookers crowded around them.

"Smell that?" Skull asked Joseph.

"It's hard not to," he answered, trying not to gag at the stench that rose up from the water.

"This is where the slimiest, grimiest bits of flotsam and jetsam are sent from our kitchen. The foulest grease. The most stale of fish."

"That's terrible!" Fleetfeet said. "You're polluting your own water!"

"Not at all!" Skull cried. "We have a few saurians who consider this mess a delicacy. They come by and gobble it all up once a week. As you can see, they're about due."

Joseph nodded. The water was turning green. He suspected that his cheeks were turning the same color.

"There will be two contests," Skull told the boys. "In each, you both will compete as a team against a team from the Black Fish. If you win *either* contest, I'll tell you where Crabb has gone."

"And if we don't?" Fleetfeet asked.

Skull shrugged. "Well, no harm will come to any of you. Despite appearances, we're a civilized lot. But, as you've mentioned, there should be some penalty for losing…hmm…"

After a moment, Skull spoke again. "How about this? If you lose, we'll tell you where Crabb is any-way—*after* you've stayed here a week, repeating these contests each night for our entertainment. Of course, by then, Lee Crabb will probably be gone from where he said he was going. But that's no concern of mine."

"We should tell him the truth," Joseph whispered. "If he knew about the map—"

"No," Fleetfeet said. "They might not believe us when we tell them the map is false. We don't want a race on our hands, with all this lot chasing after Crabb and the map, too!"

Skull leaned forward. "Must I remind you gentlemen that there is no need for discussion at this point? You already agreed to the contests."

"That's right," an old man piped up.

Something about the old man's voice sounded familiar to Joseph and Fleetfeet. They turned and looked but did not recognize the man's crooked posture, long white hair, and thick white beard.

"Let's get on with it," Joseph said, turning back.

"The rules are simple," explained Skull. "The two of you must walk out to the end of this dock, then turn around and walk back. After you've tried, we'll let *our* team have a go."

"That's it?" Joseph asked.

"Well, just another thing…one must balance on the shoulders of the other!"

Fleetfeet laughed. "That's *nothing!*"

"Don't be so sure!" called a female voice.

Joseph and Fleetfeet turned to see Teegan moving in the crowd. She was now dressed as the serving maid had been, with a billowy white shirt and red skirt. Her black hair was washed and perfumed, but there was nothing dainty about her. She appeared ready for any challenge.

"The way I see it," Teegan said, "I think they mean for you to walk the plank!"

"You might want to heed the lass," said Skull.

"Fah!" said Joseph, quoting his mentor.

"Yes, fah!" Fleetfeet chimed in.

The dome-headed dinosaur crouched and Joseph stood upon his shoulders. Fleetfeet walked ahead with confidence to spare.

The planks beneath his feet, however, were not so assured. This part of the dock had been built on floating barrels and each step brought a terrible tipping movement. The boys were nearly thrown into the smelly water right away!

"Keep it steady down there!" Joseph called.

"I'm trying!" Fleetfeet replied. "Why couldn't it have been a wrestling contest? I'm good at that!"

The Stegoceras walked carefully along. The planks moaned and threatened to give way, forcing him to shift his weight from side to side just to keep from falling.

All might have been well, but Joseph kept trying to direct Fleetfeet. "Not that way!" he cried.

As Fleetfeet took more tentative steps, he began telling Joseph what to do. "Shift your weight, Joseph! Aren't you watching!"

"Watching! You're not balancing properly!"

For the spectators, it was a comical sight. The pair looked like two ill-matched dance partners.

"All we need is some music!" Skull cried.

Roars of laughter met each of Fleetfeet and Joseph's steps. As the two teetered and swayed in odd ways to keep from falling, everyone laughed.

Everyone except Teegan. *If only they'd work together,* she thought, *instead of each trying to claim the role of leader.* It seemed to Teegan as if the two were focused on competing *against* each other rather than *for* the completion of the task!

"I know what I'm doing!" barked Fleetfeet.

"We'd have been in the drink five times by now if not for me!" Joseph returned.

Fleetfeet took another step. The board beneath him cracked. He almost had enough time to hop to a different board, but he was too busy telling Joseph which way to lean. Meanwhile, Joseph hadn't bothered leaning because he was too busy directing Fleetfeet where to step next.

Fleetfeet's claw struck a slick board, and he cried out as both he and Joseph tumbled from their feet into the foul, stinking water!

The splash raised a wave of gunk and caused a foul odor to drift back to the denizens of the Black Fish. But no one seemed put out. They were too busy enjoying the show.

Joseph and Fleetfeet were about to climb from the waters when they saw the arm-wrestling duo from the tavern walking the plank. The pair moved in unison, one trusting the other, both working together to safely walk out and back.

It was over. Joseph and Fleetfeet had *lost* the first of the competitions.

Climbing out of the water, Joseph turned to Fleetfeet. "I hope the next event *is* wrestling. One sniff of us and our opponents will instantly faint!"

The boys were taken away to have their clothing and bodies hosed down and dried off. When they got back, a trampoline was in place. The human and saurian team were already on it.

"I say, you don't mind if we go first this time, do you?" asked the burly man.

"Please," Joseph said.

He and Fleetfeet watched as men with ladders fixed an array of lines high above their heads. On each of these lines was placed a small cork fishing float. No one explained the object of the game, but it soon became clear.

The burly man and his saurian friend bounced on the trampoline, each grabbing fishing floats from the lower lines. Then a curious thing happened. The saurian began bouncing in place, allowing the human to rise higher and higher. The man was able to snatch every fishing float except the last, which hung twenty feet in the air.

The duo stepped down to a thunderous roar of applause. The floats were reset, then Skull turned to the lads and said, "Your turn."

Joseph spoke to Fleetfeet. "Remember, all we need is to win one contest and they'll let us go."

"Easy for you to say."

The two climbed onto the trampoline and started bouncing to get their bearings. Suddenly, Teegan jumped on, too!

"What are you doing?" Fleetfeet asked.

"Advising you!" announced Teegan. "You must do what they did. One can help propel the other."

"But which of us does the hard work and which gets the glory?" Joseph asked.

"If you win, we'll *all* get the glory of leaving this place tonight."

"Good point," Fleetfeet said.

Joseph sighed. "It was my fault we lost the last one. Fleetfeet, you decide. I'll do what you say."

"Well…I have more weight to me," the dome-headed saurian reasoned. "I should be the anchor, and you should snatch the floats."

"Agreed."

Teegan hopped off the trampoline and watched. Joseph and Fleetfeet each claimed a few of the prizes from the lower lines. Then Fleetfeet became the "shooter" and Joseph started flying higher with every bounce.

"Well, look at that," said the burly man. "Team-work. I didn't think they had it in them!"

Joseph snatched prize after prize until only the last float remained. But, try as he might, he couldn't reach high enough to grab the last float.

Seeing his partner's distress, Fleetfeet struck harder at the trampoline, but it did no good. Then he re-called a trick he'd learned from a cousin long ago. He flipped himself and started striking the trampoline with his hard, domed head.

It was working! Joseph rose higher and higher,

until finally he snatched the last prize—and won! Applause rose from the crowd. Joseph and Fleetfeet climbed down on wobbly legs.

"Sauropolis," Skull said, patting each of them on the back. "Lee Crabb went there to meet with a gentleman named Kaluta."

"Thank you," said the boys breathlessly.

The boys were about to depart with Teegan when Fleetfeet turned suddenly. "By the way, Skull, was Crabb alone?" he asked.

"He was alone when he came here. Why?"

"No reason," Joseph said quickly, exchanging glances with Fleetfeet. They knew Crabb had a partner. But *who* could it be? This "Kaluta" perhaps? Or was Kaluta a buyer of the map?

After the trio departed, something very strange happened. The old man in the dark cloak removed his white wig and beard. Then he straightened his crooked back.

It was Townsend.

"You've all done well," he said to the group of scalawags. "I doubt that even my *partner* in this little venture could be more pleased."

Together, they all laughed and laughed

CHAPTER 11

Sauropolis was unlike any place on Dinotopia that Joseph and Fleetfeet had ever seen. The buildings were taller and more ornately decorated than most other cities. Arches stretched across walkways. Tall, thin spires with bulbous heads reached into the skies.

The city streets were more hectic than those of Waterfall City. But the people were the same. Warm and friendly. It took little time for Joseph, Fleetfeet, and Teegan to find the house of the man Skull had mentioned.

Not surprisingly, the house was massive. Kaluta was clearly a man of some importance in the city. Fleetfeet knocked on the door. It opened to reveal a smiling red-haired boy and a collection of playful saurians who were racing through the main hall.

The boy looked at the visitors from horn to tail

and said, "My goodness! The three of you look to be in the horsetails. May I help you?"

"We need to speak with a gentle soul named Kaluta," Joseph said.

"This is his home, which he shares with all his lost boys," the lad said. "Come and be welcome. Kaluta is in the garden. I'll take you there."

Joseph, Fleetfeet, and Teegan were led through the elegant manse. Beautiful vases and crystalline sculptures sat everywhere. Joseph watched the young ones having fun and was struck by the way not a single item was knocked down or broken, despite their high-spirited play.

Fleetfeet noticed how pleasant the household seemed. On the trip here, he'd talked with Joseph and Teegan about Kaluta's possible role in this map business.

The trio suspected Kaluta of being either Crabb's mysterious partner or simply a buyer for the map. But it seemed absurd to Fleetfeet that someone who lived in such a tranquil place as this would be skulking around with Crabb. Kaluta *had* to be a buyer. Yet…why would someone living *here* desire a map that led off the island?

The group was taken through a wide set of double doors into a breathtaking garden. Statues of humans and dinosaurs working and playing together rose from beds of exotic flowers.

A handsome, long-haired man with bold dark eyes

stood up the moment he saw his visitors He smiled warmly

"Thank you, Michael," Kaluta said. The red-haired boy waved and departed. "Now, what can I do for you kind souls? Something to eat? At least feel free to set down your burdens."

The three had been carting around their back-packs of supplies for so long they barely even noticed them anymore.

"Tell me," Kaluta said "How can I help you?"

"We're looking for a man named " began Joseph, but before he could finish, a figure emerged through the double doors

He was an older man, dressed in a soot-colored frock with baggy pants and a tall, rumpled hat lined with shells and claws. In his hand was a smelly cigar

"Lee Crabb!" exclaimed Fleetfeet

Without a word, Crabb bolted. The trio immedi-ately raced after him.

Crabb led them on a merry chase through the manse. Although he was older and a bit slower, he was much craftier and not above smashing a vase or over-turning a sculpture to slow down or trip up his young pursuers.

Then he burst out of the front door and raced into the street, disappearing into the crowd.

The trio arrived a second too late to see which way he'd gone. But all was not lost. Fleetfeet sniffed the air and pointed.

As they ran, Fleetfeet said, "So long as Crabb keeps smoking those putrid cigars, I'll always know right where to find him."

"I'm surprised you can still smell anything after that dip in the pool you and Joseph took back at the Black Fish," Teegan said as she ran beside the boys.

"Don't remind me," Joseph said.

They followed Crabb through an archway leading to an underground cavern filled with mineral springs. Humans and saurians bathed here to enjoy the water's healing properties.

Fleetfeet ran toward a bulky man wearing only a towel. "You!" cried Fleetfeet. The trail created by Crabb's cigar had led right here. But when the man looked over his shoulder, Fleetfeet saw that he wasn't Crabb. He'd just been holding Crabb's cigar!

"Yes?" asked the man. "Tell me, please: What am I supposed to do with this now?"

Teegan immediately stepped up. "The man who gave you the cigar—where did he go?"

The man pointed to an exit at the far side of the cavern. The trio raced ahead. The exit led to a tunnel that rose up back to the street.

"Now what are we going to do?" Joseph asked. "Lee Crabb could be anywhere!"

"Do you think he'll go back to Kaluta?" Fleetfeet asked.

"Joseph," Teegan said, "you double back there. I'll stay with Fleetfeet and search the city."

"Shouldn't I be the one to—" Joseph began.

"Just go!" Teegan said, taking Fleetfeet's arm and hurrying into the crowd.

Sighing, Joseph headed the other way.

It wasn't long before Fleetfeet spotted Crabb's distinctive hat rising above the crowd of humans and saurians clogging the street.

"You go ahead," Teegan said. "Circle around ahead of him. I'll try to drive him to you."

"What if it's another trick?" Fleetfeet asked.

Teegan shrugged. "What if it's not?"

It turned out that Teegan was right. She slipped through the crowd and soon came upon Crabb. He gasped as he saw her and ran, pushing over carts and shoving saurians into her way to make his escape.

The moment he saw Fleetfeet closing on him from the other direction, he turned and ran into a building that looked like an ancient temple.

Fleetfeet and Teegan followed Crabb inside. A lush theater was within, with crimson and black decor. Upon a stage, a group of dinosaurs wearing strange masks performed a graceful pantomime. A group of musicians played a haunting melody.

Crabb had vanished once again.

"There must be a hundred people watching the play," Teegan whispered.

"All he'd have to do is take off his hat and we'd never be able to spot him," Fleetfeet said.

Suddenly, a gong rang out.

"Ah! My ears!" someone cried

Teegan looked in the direction of the yell and saw Lee Crabb rising up from behind the gong. He fled toward an exit. Teegan and Fleetfeet did, too.

The chase continued through narrow back alleys where saurians sat with blankets covered in exotic jewelry They arrived at a dock where festival-goers lined the street and a host of ships was sailing along, carrying lanterns

Teegan and Fleetfeet failed to see Crabb anywhere—until Teegan noticed one of the lantern boats heading away from all the others. Lee Crabb stood upon it, waving good-bye!

Teegan looked for a boat they could use to chase him, but had no luck. Crabb got away.

Fleetfeet and Teegan could do nothing more, so they returned to Kaluta's house. That's where they found Joseph, talking with the man in his library.

"...and you see, I have no real desire to live anywhere but Dinotopia," Kaluta was explaining to Joseph. "But before I was shipwrecked here, I was engaged to be married. I thought I might leave the island long enough to find my beloved and bring her here, so that we both might enjoy this place of wonders."

"Joseph," said Fleetfeet softly. "Did you ask him about the map?"

Joseph nodded.

Kaluta looked at the three worried youths before him. "Now...do not be in the horsetails. I will do all I can to help you find Lee Crabb."

The trio sighed with relief.

"I spoke with him earlier today to discuss terms for the map," explained Kaluta. "He was returning to lead me to it when you arrived. When we spoke, he mentioned two places we would visit. The map is likely hidden in one of those places." Kaluta paused a moment. "Yes, you must find Crabb. The poor man has no idea the map is false. I'm sure of it."

"So where are we heading?" Teegan asked.

Kaluta looked thoughtfully at her. "Crabb mentioned a set of ruins far distant. But his first port of call was to be the Caverns of the Winds. I'll call my wagons together. You must leave at once!"

CHAPTER 12

The Caverns of the Winds were located in the mountains outside of Sauropolis.

Kaluta had loaned Joseph, Fleetfeet, and Teegan two wagons and some trusted members of his household to help them find their destination. But even from a distance, the trio could have located the cavern entrance by sound. The howling winds that had given the caverns their name could be heard for miles.

When Kaluta's wagons finally arrived, the three friends climbed down from their cushioned seats. Before them, the mouth of the cavern seemed gigantic.

"There's no wind blowing," Joseph said. "Yet I can hear the roars coming from the cavern."

"Everything has a spirit," said Llewlyn, a wise Avaceratops. "The earth beneath us. The stones ahead. I've heard it said that this is the meeting place for all the winds there are. Monsoons come here to greet their fellows—tornadoes, hurricanes, every wind from the fiercest gale to the slightest breeze. They all gather here."

"Will the winds sweep us away?" Teegan asked with concern.

Llewlyn laughed. "The winds are gentle to visitors. What you hear are their echoes. The truly great winds lie far below. They allow no one to visit them."

"What about torches to light our way?" Fleetfeet asked. "Won't the winds put them out?"

"We've brought lanterns for you," Llewlyn said. "Be careful to protect them from the harshest of the winds, and you will be fine."

A young saurian brought three lit lanterns from the supply wagon and handed them out.

"Breathe deep," Llewlyn said.

"Seek peace," Teegan answered brightly. She turned to Joseph and whispered, "How was that? Am I getting it?"

"Like a true Dinotopian," he said with a smile of pride for her. Joseph had been teaching Teegan Dinotopian sayings and customs during their travels. And, in that moment, he realized something about himself: he really enjoyed seeing someone learn—and knowing he'd had something to do with it.

"Hey, what is that thing?" asked Fleetfeet just before they entered the caverns.

Joseph saw an object lying in the half-light near the cavern mouth. He crouched down over it.

"Hmm. Have a smell of this, Fleetfeet."

"Awful," said the Stegoceras, rubbing his snout. "Yes, that's Crabb's cigar, all right…"

"Shall we?" asked Teegan.

The trio continued inside. The cavern was cooler than any of them had expected. Joseph had to brace himself as the winds cut through him.

The winds seemed almost alive, passing around each of them like the icy hands of someone without sight who wished to know the features of his visitors. Their lantern flames violently flickered as they withstood this odd greeting.

Then, after a few minutes of intense roaring, the winds abruptly retreated. Luckily, the group's lanterns remained lit.

They pressed deeper into the cavern and approached a juncture—it was the first of many. Llewlyn had already warned that there would be such forks, so they formed a plan to always take the right-hand path. This way, at least, they could find their way back.

"In Scotland," Teegan said, to pass the time as they walked, "we believe that where any two roads cross is a special place."

"How so?" asked Fleetfeet.

"If you stand there at the right time," explained Teegan, "you might be able to see into other worlds."

"Sounds like your floating city, Fleetfeet," teased Joseph.

"There were many nights when I'd stay up until

midnight and stand at a crossroads, longing to glimpse the Land of Faeries, or some other amazing place," said Teegan, lost in the memory. "It seems I've waited all my life to see a wonderful new land. Faith, I swear this isle of yours is such a thing. A crossroads where worlds meet. Pure magic!"

Joseph and Fleetfeet smiled at Teegan's story as their walk continued. After a time, the group's enthusiasm was beginning to give way to worry.

"So if Lee Crabb is here, what's our plan for dealing with him?" Teegan asked.

"I'm certain we will just need to explain the situation," Fleetfeet said.

Joseph agreed. "I'm sure he'll listen to reason."

"Reason!" declared Teegan. "From what you've told me about Crabb, he hardly seems the type."

"Well," said Joseph, "I can't believe that he actually *knows* that the map is no good. Once he realizes that, he'll hand it right over."

"I hope you're right," Teegan said.

The winds were becoming harsh again. The trio had to speak louder just to be heard.

"Do you think we should turn back?" Teegan asked. "We've been at this for some time now and we haven't seen anything. Lee Crabb may have been taking other paths—"

"Look!" Fleetfeet said, pointing at a flicker of light in the far distance. It suddenly rounded a curve and disappeared.

"Let's go!" cried Joseph.

The chase seemed to go on forever. They never caught more than a glimpse of the figure they were after. They couldn't even tell if Crabb knew he was being followed!

The caverns split, and split again, offering junctures that held two, three, and sometimes more choices. But the light ahead always stayed in view, so their choices were made for them.

Then, suddenly, the light vanished. The trio kept running, but the next time they came to a juncture, they had no idea which way to go.

"We should split up," Fleetfeet said. "There are three tunnels before us, and three of us. If we each take a tunnel, at least *one* will find Crabb!"

"Maybe," said Joseph. "Or maybe we'll all just end up lost."

"Don't you think that's what he was trying to do?" Teegan asked. "Confuse us? Get us lost?"

Joseph's shoulders sagged. "I don't even know how to get back. Do either of you?"

Fleetfeet shook his head. "We're lost."

"Nonsense," said Teegan. "I kept notes of every move we made."

"Where?" Joseph asked.

Teegan tapped the side of her head. "Right here. I can get us back. I never forget anything."

"What do you think?" Joseph asked Fleetfeet. "Should we turn around or press on?"

"I say we keep going!" Fleetfeet cried.

Teegan shook her head. "The way these tunnels connect, Lee Crabb could have doubled back easily. He could be long gone from here while we're still arguing!"

"A little farther," Joseph said. "Feel the breeze? It's warmer now. It's been getting warmer as we've been coming this way. Let's see what's taking away the chill. If Lee Crabb has the advantage you say, Teegan, then we'll never catch him today, anyway."

"But Llewlyn guards the entrance," Fleetfeet said.

"He guards *one* entrance. Unfortunately, there may be others. And Crabb may have left a cigar at that entrance just to put us on a false trail."

"All right," Teegan said. "A little farther..."

The breezes grew warmer as they went on. Even the howling winds seemed less harsh and more inviting, like a siren's call.

Suddenly, a flicker of light came from somewhere ahead. The trio turned a corner and saw where the warmth was coming from.

They stepped into a cozy chamber lit by a golden blaze in its center. The walls had been carved into the forms of saurians and something like a nest had been created in one side.

Throughout the chamber, dozens of cracked-open eggshells lay scattered. A man kneeled before one of them. He rose and came forward. The fire behind him cast him in silhouette.

"We have you now," Joseph said as the figure approached.

"There's nowhere to go," Fleetfeet added.

Teegan stood at the ready, beside her friends.

Finally, the figure revealed himself.

But it was *not* Lee Crabb.

"Hello, lads," said the familiar voice.

"Townsend!" Joseph cried.

"The one you told me about?" Teegan asked suspiciously. "Steelgaze's friend?"

"I am Steelgaze's friend, that is true," Townsend said.

"He must be trying to find Lee Crabb, too!" Fleetfeet cried.

"Lee Crabb?" Townsend said. "No. Why would I be looking for him? More to the point—why are you?"

Teegan leaped forward. "You're sure you're not just *covering* for Mr. Crabb? Keeping us busy and giving him a chance to escape?"

"Teegan!" Joseph exclaimed. "Townsend's a friend. He'd never be in league with Crabb. I guarantee it!"

She frowned. "If you say so…"

"Lads, I asked you a question," Townsend said. "These caverns can be dangerous. Why are you here? And what's your friend talking about? Why would I be in league with Crabb?"

Joseph and Fleetfeet regarded one another. Steelgaze had instructed them to be careful in telling anyone of their quest. But this was Townsend, one of Steelgaze's oldest friends. And it was looking as if they could use some help.

"Steelgaze sent us to the Time Towers to find an old map," Joseph said.

"The map showed a route off the island," Fleetfeet said.

"But it's not a true route anymore, if it ever was. When we got to its hiding place, we learned that Lee Crabb had taken it."

Townsend nodded grimly and looked to Teegan. "With someone's help?"

"Aye," she whispered.

"Now we have to find him before he can create any mischief with the map. Will you help us?"

Townsend didn't answer. Instead, he turned to the young woman accompanying the boys. "And who would you be?" Townsend asked.

The young woman bowed. "Teegan MacGregor. At your service."

Townsend looked at all three of them. "If you'd really like to be at my service, you'd listen to my tale, just as I've listened to yours."

"Yes," Joseph said.

"Please," said Fleetfeet.

"A young dinosaur has lost his way and left the Rainy Basin," Townsend said. "I've followed him here, though I can see he's long gone. This place was a Hatchery once. The golden flame you see is perpetual—it never goes out. I couldn't tell you why. What's important is that the dinosaur I'm looking for is frightened and may cause trouble without meaning to."

"What's the Rainy Basin?" Teegan asked.

Townsend looked at her. "Are you a dolphinback?"

"Dolphins saved me, yes."

"How long ago?"

"Just yesterday," said Teegan.

"She wanted to come with us and help," said Joseph. "We're taking her to Waterfall City once we have the map."

Townsend nodded. "The Rainy Basin is where the Tyrannosauruses and other noble, meat-eating dinosaurs live. They generally prefer to keep to themselves, and we have a tendency to let them. But at times, travel through the Rainy Basin is necessary and when that is so, precautions must be taken: armored dinosaur escorts and fish to keep the Tyrannosauruses and their companions happy and distracted. If one of these Rainy Basin saurians was lost and on his own, confused and frightened—"

"I understand," Teegan said. "This land is not without its dangers."

"What place is?" Townsend said.

"How could such a thing happen?" Joseph asked.

"That's not really important. All that matters is that it has happened and now it must be dealt with. I have some ideas about what to do with this wayward soul once I find him, but I won't be able to accomplish them on my own. Would any of you be willing to help me?"

Joseph felt torn. He understood the importance of Townsend's mission. And yet...

"I made a promise to Steelgaze," Joseph said.

"So did I," Fleetfeet said.

Townsend nodded. "I understand you wish to honor your word to your teacher." Then he paused and spoke again. "How about this. One of you comes to help me while the other searches for Crabb and the map. How would that be?"

"Well..." Joseph said.

"Which of us?" Fleetfeet asked.

"Either," said Townsend. "The two of you should decide."

Joseph suddenly envisioned returning home and finding Steelgaze showering Fleetfeet with praise for finding the map, while barely noticing him. The thought shamed him and he tried to turn it away.

A similar image was racing through Fleetfeet's mind. But, in his imagination, it was Joseph who was the proud victor, and he, Fleetfeet, who would have to follow in Joseph's shadow.

"I wonder," Townsend said. "Is it possible that the two of you are hesitating because you know that you need to *work together* to find the map? That neither of you feels confident enough in his own abilities to take on the task himself?"

"Confidence is one thing neither of these young knights is lacking!" Teegan piped up.

"I could do it myself," Joseph said. "No question."

"The same with me!" Fleetfeet said, placing his snout firmly in the air.

"See?" said Teegan.

"Well, then," said Townsend, "if you don't *need* to work together, what difference does it make if only one of you fulfills the quest instead of both? Steelgaze would certainly understand."

Joseph and Fleetfeet stared at each other in silence.

"I suppose I do need Fleetfeet's help," said Joseph. "Lee Crabb is clever and quick."

"Yes," Fleetfeet said. "Working together, the two of us have a much better chance of finding Crabb and getting the map back."

"Besides," Joseph said. "Fleetfeet would be lost without me."

"Not likely," Fleetfeet said. "You're the one who always looks to me for—"

"That's enough," Townsend said, shaking his head. Then Teegan spoke. "*I'll* go with you."

Joseph and Fleetfeet both looked thunderstruck.

"You'd leave us?" Joseph asked.

"I'm not leaving you," Teegan said. "I'm joining Townsend. If either of you wants to come along, that would be wonderful."

"We can't—" Joseph said.

"Steelgaze—" Fleetfeet began.

"We should go," Townsend said. "I know the way out of here."

"I'll miss you," Joseph said.

"Me too," added Fleetfeet.

"I'll miss you both. But sometimes we just have to do what our hearts tell us. Don't we?" asked Teegan as they all left the golden chamber.

The boys didn't answer.

CHAPTER 13

Fleetfeet and Joseph were soon focused on the second place that Lee Crabb was supposed to be heading: the Ruins of New Chandaran.

On the wagon ride there, the boys missed Teegan. The pair sang songs with Llewlyn and the other saurians. They told stories and played games. But, despite these distractions, a feeling of heaviness stayed with Joseph and Fleetfeet.

"She was disappointed with us," Fleetfeet said.

"No," Joseph said, far too quickly. "She was just concerned about the lost dinosaur from the Rainy Basin and those who might cross his path."

"I suppose…"

Night fell and Llewlyn approached with sad news. "Lads, one of our group has fallen ill, so we must turn back tonight. But don't despair. The ruins are only a few more miles."

After the caravan departed, Joseph and Fleetfeet made camp. The next morning they began to hike toward the ruins. It wasn't long before the crumbling walls of the once-great New Chandaran were in sight.

From a distance, New Chandaran looked like an ancient fort. They drew closer to see huge statues of crowned saurians rising behind the towering walls like stone lookouts.

The boys passed through a large set of opened gates and walked into the deserted city. A wide street stretched before them. It was completely lined with stone sphinxes that had saurian faces. Many were crumbling, but some were still whole.

Bits of pottery lay about, decorated with images of birds and animals. Figurines modeled from clay lay half-buried in the ruins. Many large sculptures stood unfinished—their backs and sides nothing but plain blocks of stone.

Colonnaded courts abounded. And everywhere were great crumbling stone pillars decorated with lotuses, ankhs, and claws.

Fleetfeet was especially absorbed in the sight.

"Fleetfeet," whispered Joseph, "it almost looks like one of your cities in the sky, fallen to earth."

Fleetfeet nodded, speechless.

It was when they passed by a large courtyard bordering a road that they saw Lee Crabb. He just stood there. He didn't bolt or try to hide. It was as if he'd been waiting for them.

In his hands was an old scroll. "There are treasures aplenty in this place," Crabb said. "You only have to know where to look."

Joseph and Fleetfeet stood with dropped jaws. Lee Crabb laughed. "Well, lads, you got me. Now the question is—can you keep me?"

Joseph studied the grizzled man in disbelief. "The map you took is dangerous," he said evenly.

"Dangerous to fools, perhaps." He looked to Fleetfeet. "To those who cannot accept what they know in their hearts to be true."

Crabb's words touched something deep within Fleetfeet. "He's just trying to confuse us. All that matters is the map."

"Yes," Joseph said. "Where is it, Crabb?"

Lee Crabb shrugged. He took off his tall cap and shook it out. "Not there." He turned out his pockets and emptied the bag he carried. "Not there either. Strange, isn't it?"

"He doesn't have it with him," Fleetfeet said.

"What have you done with it?" Joseph asked.

"I gave it to a friend," Crabb said. "Someone who's hurrying back to Waterfall City with it." Crabb sat down on a rock and grinned. "So, please, lads. Take your time with me. It'll only help my friend, who'll auction the map to the highest bidder and split the profits with me."

"I don't believe you," Joseph said.

"Neither do I," Fleetfeet added. "Everyone knows

how much you wish to leave Dinotopia. If you had a map in your hands that showed a way off the island, you'd never part with it."

"Not unless you knew the map was false," said Joseph, beginning to understand. "That's it, isn't it? I didn't want to believe anyone in this good land could have such low motives, but turning a profit *is* all that matters to you, isn't it?"

"I look out for myself," Crabb said. "If I didn't, who would?"

"Everyone on this island!" Fleetfeet cried. "The hand of friendship's been offered to you many times, and you always turn it away."

"Are you offering me that hand now?" Crabb asked, nodding toward Fleetfeet's claw.

"Of course," Joseph said. "You could be a hero. We'd make sure everyone knows that you found the map and destroyed it."

"So I could be in everybody's scroll, is that what you're offering?"

"Yes," Joseph said.

"Sounds like a bit of a fib," Crabb said. "And I know about fibs. In fact, I may've told you one."

"What do you mean?" Joseph asked.

Crabb shrugged. "It's possible that I don't have a partner in this at all—"

"We *know* you have a partner," Joseph said.

Fleetfeet nodded. "You couldn't have gotten into that room at the Time Towers alone."

"So you say," Crabb muttered. "Still, I may have hidden the map here in these ruins. Or somewhere else. And unless the two o' ya plan on devoting your lives to watching my every move, you'll never know for sure. Unless, o' course, what I'm telling ya *now* is the fib and my partner really is taking the map to Waterfall City."

The boys exchanged helpless glances.

"It's hard, isn't it?" asked Crabb. "Not knowing what to believe."

Suddenly, Fleetfeet touched Joseph's arm. "Clawbrother, look!"

On the twisting road ahead, a group of humans and saurians came into view. They walked with their heads down and their shoulders slumped, as if they carried burdens far weightier than the bags strung across their backs.

A wagon with a rickety wheel came into view next. It was pulled by a Bactrosaurus who lumbered on with leaden steps. As the procession came closer, Joseph called, "Sing and it will go away!"

The wizened, stoop-shouldered man in the lead looked at Joseph strangely. "Kind words, lad. But a song won't give us back what we've lost."

"What happened?" Fleetfeet asked.

A Euoplocephalus stepped forward. "It's good that you asked because we can warn you. If you have plans of traveling to the village of Tuckford, you may first wish to consider the risk."

"Why?" asked Joseph. "I don't understand."

"Ever been through the dangers of the Rainy Basin?" the man asked. "Well, if you haven't, then you can spare yourself the journey and travel to Tuckford instead. A dweller from that place has taken roost in our Tuckford. Or, I should say, what's *left* of our Tuckford."

"The dinosaur that Townsend told us about," Joseph said.

"What dinosaur?" Crabb asked. "What the blazes are you people going on about?"

Fleetfeet told Crabb the whole story.

"Ha!" Crabb barked. "It wouldn't be me, risking my neck to try and get that beastie back home. No, sir, it would *not.*"

Joseph ignored Crabb and looked to the refugees from Tuckford. "Did any of you see a man traveling with a pretty dark-haired girl?"

"They were recent arrivals in the village when we were on our way out," said the man.

The Euoplocephalus nodded. "We tried to warn them that there was danger, but they stayed anyway. Would any of you like to join us?"

"Not I," said Crabb. "I've got my future all *mapped* out, you might say." He began to laugh.

Joseph and Fleetfeet glared at Crabb. Then they turned to the Euoplocephalus. They thanked him for his kind offer but declined.

Slowly, the group moved on.

"We made the wrong choice yesterday," Joseph said. "Teegan and Townsend needed us."

"What about Crabb?"

Joseph shook his head. "We'll deal with him later. What else can we do?"

"Lots o' things, lads," Crabb piped in. "But you can't do 'em all at once. More's the pity for you—and more's the *profit* for me."

Joseph and Fleetfeet set out in the direction of Tuckford. Crabb watched them go. He sighed and then an odd smile crossed his grizzled face.

A part of Lee Crabb actually admired them. He'd once had the fires of youth in him, too. And he hadn't always been thought of as a bad fellow.

"Ah, well," he mumbled as he rose from his perch. Then he tucked his book in his bag and began preparations for following the boys.

Meanwhile, in the village of Tuckford, Teegan and Townsend were preparing a trap.

When they'd first arrived, they found many of the villagers had already fled. But some had stayed behind. Townsend identified the lost dinosaur as a young male Albertosaurus—a carnivore cousin of the Tyrannosaurus.

Three evenings before, the dinosaur had come through the village on a rampage, terrifying its inhabitants, then retreating back to the jungle. The next day, the villagers came up with an idea. They left baskets of fish in a clearing.

It seemed to work. For the last two evenings, the Albertosaurus had eaten the fish and gone back to its hiding place, avoiding the village.

But supplies were running low. So Townsend and Teegan devised a plan for the village. A pit was dug and carefully covered up. Baskets of fish sat upon the covering. Now everyone was waiting at the edge of the clearing to see if their trap would work.

"Tell me more about this Steelgaze fellow," Teegan said to Townsend as the two watched the clearing from behind a wide tree. "I can tell that Joseph and Fleetfeet love him very much. But he sounds like something of a stern taskmaster."

"He is that," Townsend said. "But there's more to him. Much more. If he didn't believe in Joseph and Fleetfeet so much, he would never push them the way he does."

"But if he thinks so highly of them, why doesn't he tell them so?"

"I could think of a thousand reasons. One is that he comes from a clan of dinosaurs that believes it is better to show such things than to say them."

"I know Joseph and Fleetfeet wish to hear words of praise from Steelgaze," Teegan said.

"Until they grow to truly believe in themselves," said Townsend, "such words will only be heard in their ears and not in their hearts. Those two may listen to Steelgaze—but they have yet to hear."

Before Teegan could say anything else, a rustling came from the bushes next to them.

"He's coming," a woman whispered.

"What will happen if the trap works?" Teegan asked Townsend.

"Once we have him contained, I'll send messengers to bring ambassadors here. They'll know how to speak to him and convince him to be led home. But right now we have to keep him from doing any more damage."

Suddenly, the ground began to shake. Teegan heard the leaves parting and looked up to see a huge dinosaur entering the clearing. The Albertosaurus stood nearly fifteen feet tall. It roared as it spotted the baskets of food that had been left for it.

"He looks like a dragon," Teegan said. "A dragon on two legs."

The Albertosaurus resembled its Tyrannosaurus cousin quite a bit, but its body was sleeker, its two-fingered hands attached to limbs longer than its cousin's stubby forelimbs. And the large skull of the Albertosaurus had a much wider muzzle, too. A muzzle that was filled with sharp dagger-like teeth!

As the wild green and black dinosaur stalked forward on powerful rear legs, its long tail helping to keep it balanced, Teegan and Townsend gasped.

It wasn't alone! Two smaller Albertosauruses walked behind it.

"Did it have babies?" Teegan whispered.

Townsend shook his head. "See the two small horns in front of the eyes, where the bright red and yellow splotches are? Only the males have those. The big one must have been searching for his brothers."

"And found them in Tuckford," Teegan said.

All three dinosaurs moved forward. The little ones ran ahead. Anxiously, Townsend scrambled from the brush and ran right into their path.

"What are you doing!" Teegan cried, following him into the clearing.

He nodded toward the trap—the giant pit covered over with wood, sticks, and grass. The food had been set in the center of the covering, so that the Albertosaurus would crash through the trap as he tried to reach it.

"I don't know if these little ones could survive the fall," Townsend said.

"So you'd rather they eat *us?*" Teegan cried.

"They won't," Townsend said.

"This is crazy!" Teegan shouted.

And then a sudden silence fell upon the clearing. Both Teegan and Townsend realized that the Albertosaurus and his younger brothers finally noticed them. They were coming closer.

"Now what?" Teegan asked.

"I'm not sure," Townsend said honestly.

"All right," Teegan said, her entire body trembling. "I have an idea. We're going to move very slowly over to the pit."

"But we can't—"

"Trust me," Teegan said, her voice shaking.

The little Albertosauruses followed Teegan's and Townsend's movements, mimicking them.

"They think it's a game," Teegan whispered. "Good." When she got to the pit's edge, she slowly reached beneath the oversize leaves. Then she picked up one of the long sticks covering the pit.

"They can snap through that in a heartbeat," Townsend warned.

"I know," Teegan said. "Now stay off to one side. We don't want the little ones falling in."

Townsend moved away from the pit.

Teegan used the long stick like a fishing pole. She hooked it under the handle of one of the food baskets and lifted it up.

All three Albertosauruses shifted their attentions to the basket.

"Gooooooooood," Teegan said. Her heart was thundering. "Aye, you fellas are just like my friend Martine's brothers, aren't you? You like to play and you like to eat."

With a sudden sharp movement, Teegan whipped the stick to one side. It sent the basket flying through the air to land at the feet of the larger Albertosaurus. The little guys sprang toward it, even as their big brother took a step back to allow them closer.

Teegan hooked her stick under the next basket. Suddenly, Townsend was beside her. He grabbed a stick and took care of the last basket at the same time that she flung hers. She heard rustling from the trees surrounding the clearing. The townsfolk were fleeing!

"Let's go!" Townsend said, taking her hand.

"No," Teegan said, pulling free. "They could still stumble into the pit. We've got to uncover it."

"We don't have time," Townsend said. "If we go now, they won't be back again until tomorrow. We can work out another plan."

Teegan wasn't listening. She was determined to uncover the pit. Growling with frustration, Townsend began to help. Together they snatched up the sticks.

Ahead, the trio of dinosaurs happily munched their dinner. Then silence returned. Teegan looked up sharply.

The dinosaurs were advancing again.

"Go!" Townsend said. "I'll draw their attention long enough for you to escape!"

Teegan shook her head. "There's one place we can go that they'd have enough sense to avoid."

"You don't mean—" Townsend began.

She did. Teegan took a running leap and jumped right into the pit!

CHAPTER 14

In a hail of broken sticks and soft leaves, Teegan plunged to the bottom of the pit. Townsend leaped in after her, landing without injury. The soft sandy earth was able to break the fall of the light humans. The younger Albertosaurus brothers may not have been as lucky.

For a few moments after landing, neither spoke. Then Teegan moaned and Townsend grunted. He looked up and saw the three dangerous carnivores peering down at them curiously.

"And we were worried about *them* getting hurt," Teegan muttered.

"Are you all right?" Townsend asked.

"I think so."

"That was a foolish thing you did. Brave, but foolish."

"You left out clever."

"Yes, well, look!" One of the smaller Albertosauruses was moving closer to the pit's edge. He looked as if he might try leaping in. "I'll have to reserve calling it 'clever' just yet…"

Suddenly, a cry came from far above. The dinosaurs looked up.

"A Skybax!" Townsend exclaimed.

"A what?"

"There!" Townsend pointed toward a breathtaking winged-shaped creature far above. A series of screeches came from the shape. The sounds drew the Albertosauruses away.

"Is that a man riding on that thing's back?" Teegan asked.

"Indeed it is," Townsend said. He'd recognized the cry of that particular Skybax. "Indeed!"

Far above, Will Denison and Cirrus flew toward the Albertosauruses. Will was a friend of the Skybax Rider Rudolfo. It was Rudolfo who asked Will and Cirrus to find the two boys who'd saved his life. He'd guessed that the boys were on a quest, and he thought they might need help.

Will had found Joseph and Fleetfeet—but instead of asking for help themselves, the boys asked Will to fly to Tuckford and see if help was needed there. And, sure enough, it was!

"Cirrus," called Will to his Skybax, "are you ready to try that trick we performed during the last Dinosaur Olympics?"

Cirrus let out a cry of enthusiasm and dove straight toward the three Albertosauruses. As they swooped down, Will freed his legs from the harness and dangled them over one side, practically within reach of the largest. The Albertosauruses looked up sharply and sprang toward Will.

"Whoa!" Will cried, slipping his feet back into the harness. A young man he'd met, named Ned LeGrange, had told Will about different forms of "trick riding" performed on horses in the States.

The Albertosauruses chased Will for several miles, then gave up. They took shelter in a cave and did not emerge again.

By the time Will and Cirrus circled back to the clearing, dozens of villagers were there, helping to raise the pair from the pit. Will saw that Joseph and Fleetfeet had just arrived and were lending their help.

Suddenly, a thundering sounded. Heavy footsteps came from beyond the jungle. *Is there another Albertosaurus?* Will wondered.

A tree fell and a strange contraption stomped into the clearing. It looked like a giant mechanical crab! And a *man* was driving it!

"Let's go see what's happening," Will said to Cirrus, who quickly landed.

Will shook his head as he saw the man stepping down from the vehicle. "Lee Crabb," called Will. He gestured at the strange crab-shaped machine. "Well, this is fitting, I suppose."

"By my stars, if it isn't Will Denison!" Crabb exclaimed. "I was remarking just a few weeks ago to my good friends Gruff and Duff that it'd been too long since I'd seen you or your dear father!"

"I'm not even going to ask," Will said, who quite readily recalled Crabb's less than admirable behavior some time ago. It had earned Crabb the constant companionship of two vigilant Stygimoloch wardens—Gruff and Duff.

"I've been behaving myself," Crabb said. "So well, in fact, that I've been granted a bit of parole, you might say!"

Joseph approached. "What is that thing? Where'd you get it?"

"It's a strutter," Fleetfeet told Joseph. "They were built here centuries ago, then abandoned."

"Very good," said Crabb. "You know something about history, do ya?"

"Where did you get it?" Will asked.

"I found it beneath those ruins where I last saw young Joseph and Fleetfeet here," Crabb said.

"The Ruins of New Chandaran," noted Fleetfeet.

"Aye," said Crabb, "the ruins have all sorts of wonderful things like this to offer the ready scavenger—*if* ya know where to scavenge! O' course, it took some time to get it working. I imagine the two o' you were practically here before I even started out. But no matter. Old Crabby there is a fast one, he is. Just as quick as that scorpion strutter I lost in the sea, but why bring *that* unfortunate incident up!"

"So why are you here?" Will asked.

"Ah!" Crabb exclaimed. "To the point. Good, lad. Well, it seems to me that the lot o' you have a problem. One that only *I* can solve. With the help of old Crabby, who's speedy enough to outrun an Albertosaurus, *and* herd one along."

"Lee—" Will began.

"Let him finish," Teegan spoke up. "These villagers are desperate."

"What a polite lass!" Crabb exclaimed. "Now, then. I'd wager that Will here followed the dinosaurs back to their hiding place. Am I right?"

Will nodded.

"I can draw them out and lead them back to the Rainy Basin," Crabb said, taking a puff on his cigar, then staring at it for a moment. "And I'll share the information. For a price."

"What's that?" Will asked.

Crabb nodded toward Joseph and Fleetfeet. "These two lads are hounding me unfairly. They think I'm up to some shady business. I want their promises that they won't bother me no more!"

"We can't," Fleetfeet blurted without thinking. But then his gaze met Joseph's.

"Look around," Joseph whispered. "We have to."

"I know," replied Fleetfeet. "But it's not fair!" he declared to Crabb.

"Haven't you ever heard that old saying?" asked Crabb. *"Fair is the advantage to those who possess it."*

Both boys had heard that saying. They'd used it themselves in competitions, throwing it at each other without thinking. Now they realized that the saying had more than one meaning. In silence Joseph and Fleetfeet looked at one another. Then they nodded, agreeing that, at this moment, the village's safety was more important than the map—and *much* more so than their ongoing competition for Steelgaze's praise.

"All right," they said together. "We agree."

By nightfall, everything was ready. Cirrus had gone to the river and helped catch more fish. Then a filled basket was left at the entrance to the cave where the dinosaurs were hiding.

Lee Crabb sat in his strutter. The villagers, along with Townsend, Joseph, Fleetfeet, and Teegan, had all taken positions in the jungle.

Finally, all three of the Albertosauruses appeared at the cave's entrance. They were about to tear into the fish when a line that had been attached to the basket was pulled taut.

The basket was yanked back a dozen feet. The dinosaurs followed it. Twice more it was pulled. Then Lee Crabb called, "Time to go home, maties!"

A soft, muffled explosion came from behind the dinosaurs. Suddenly, a smell that made Fleetfeet dizzy rushed up into the night air. The dinosaurs fled the smell—just as Crabb said they would.

More soft pops were heard as buckets filled with smelly herbs and leaves were set on fire. The buckets had been laid in a trail in the direction of the Rainy

Basin. Before long, the entire jungle smelled like Crabb's cigar!

Crabb took a deep breath and laughed. "Now that's what I call a fine smell!"

But the Albertosauruses didn't agree. They were led along the path, fleeing the smoke with the acrid odor, until they ran right past Crabb and his strutter.

Then Crabb turned the lights on and set the sunstone-powered machine in motion. It raced after the dinosaurs, hurling stinking piles of smoking herbs their way. With the Crabb-driven strutter herding them, the dinosaurs had little desire to stray from the proper path home!

Soon, Crabb and the dinosaurs vanished into the night. Will and Cirrus flew off in their direction.

"Now what?" Joseph asked Fleetfeet.

The Stegoceras shrugged. "Now we go back to Steelgaze and tell him we failed."

Teegan heard this. "Failed?" she said. "How can you say that? These people are safe now, and they might not be, except for your sending Will and Cirrus to help! And *you* were the reason Crabb helped, too! You even worked with the villagers to help make Tuckford safe again!"

Joseph and Fleetfeet just shook their heads.

"The map is still out there," said Joseph.

"Yes," agreed Fleetfeet. "We failed."

CHAPTER 15

The next day's journey back to Waterfall City was a long one. By the time the four travelers reached the cliffs overlooking the magnificent city, all any of them wanted to do was sleep—though it was still early in the day.

Teegan's spirits were lifted by her first flight with a Wing Ambassador. She was thrilled by her first glimpse of this breathtaking city, which was criss-crossed with crystal blue canals and built on the brink of a spectacular waterfall.

Even Joseph and Fleetfeet enjoyed the ride, though their joy soon fled as they thought about facing Steel-gaze and telling him of their failure.

Once they reached the city, the boys walked ahead of Teegan and Townsend.

"Steelgaze will never be proud of us now," Joseph said sadly.

Fleetfeet nodded. "He'll *never* think we're ready to crack through the shell."

"If only we'd trusted more people with the truth," said Joseph. "Asked for more help along the way."

"But Steelgaze told us not to tell anyone—"

"Remember his *exact* words: *'Be careful* in telling anyone.' Don't you see? We should have judged better whether or not to ask for help—"

"Maybe you're right," admitted Fleetfeet. "I guess we got caught up in the competition. We were too concerned about besting each other—"

"And, the truth is, neither of us wanted to share the glory. Each of us wanted to prove that he was better for the job—"

"And, now, look at us. We've completely failed—"

"Fleetfeet, look!" Joseph cried, cutting him off.

On the street ahead was Lee Crabb. He saw them, tipped his hat, and swaggered off. And under his arm was a gold rectangular box!

"The map!" Fleetfeet said. "He has it with him!"

"But we promised not to interfere," moaned Joseph.

A voice came from behind them. "*I* didn't."

The boys spun to see Teegan grinning at them. She bolted toward Crabb, whose smug expression turned to one of alarm. He ran from her.

Townsend was instantly beside the boys. "Don't you think you should make sure your friend is going to be all right?"

"The map!" Joseph said without hesitation. "It's in that box!"

"What box?" asked Townsend.

"*I'll* explain," Fleetfeet said. "Joseph, you go ahead and watch over Teegan."

"But—" Joseph began.

"I'm faster than you," Fleetfeet explained. "I'll catch up."

This time, Joseph didn't argue. He ran after Teegan. She was very close to the fleeing man. And Joseph was soon right behind her.

They chased Crabb from the Parade Plaza into the Hedge Maze, where the greens had been carefully clipped and sculpted to look like saurians of all species.

Joseph lost sight of both Crabb and Teegan. Suddenly, he turned a corner in the vast maze and found himself face-to-face with Teegan. Mocking laughter sounded from somewhere outside the maze.

Teegan and Joseph found their way out in time to see Fleetfeet approaching. "I saw which way he went," said the saurian. "Come on!"

They caught sight of him on the boardwalk that ran parallel to the Ichthyosaur Canal.

"He's going to cross the Serenade Bridge!" Joseph said. "If I swim the canal, I can be on the other side, waiting for him!"

"Good plan!" Fleetfeet said.

Joseph leaped into the water while Teegan and

125

Fleetfeet attempted to herd Crabb across the bridge. But at the last second, Crabb made a sharp left instead of a right and ran down the street behind the Musicians' Inn.

Joseph emerged on the other side of the canals, cold and soaking wet. He saw his friends signal him that Crabb had changed course and ran to the Serenade Bridge.

"He's got nowhere to go!" cried Fleetfeet, hurrying after Crabb.

"Don't be so sure," Teegan said, pointing at a line of rafts in the distance. Crabb leaped upon one and took it across the Mosasaur Harbor.

Joseph was all the way across the Serenade Bridge when he saw his friends running his way. His shoulders slumped as he looked to the harbor, where they were pointing. Crabb's raft was moving quickly.

"We can swim across to the Concert Hall!" Joseph cried, pointing at a large columned building in the distance.

"You just want us to get as wet as you are!" Fleetfeet responded.

Frowning, Teegan turned and pushed the dinosaur into the water. Then she leaped in after him.

"What'd you do that for?" Fleetfeet asked.

"Actions speak louder than words," she said. "Come on!"

All three swam across the harbor. Crabb's raft passed between them. The grizzled man didn't smile as he saw the youths swimming his way.

By the time the trio reached the Concert Hall, Crabb was docking near Juggler's Plaza. He bolted in the direction of the library.

The trio cut through the hall and emerged out the back just in time to see Crabb heading through the thirty-foot doors of the library.

Joseph, Fleetfeet, and Teegan knew they were making quite a show as they followed him inside. They were so wet they ended up skidding along the slick floors, and Joseph actually fell on his face. But he sprang right up again.

They followed Crabb through the library, to the high wall behind where more long rafts and sea-shell gondolas were kept. There were only two crafts left.

Crabb leaped into a seashell gondola and departed. The trio grabbed the last craft left, a long raft, and gave chase.

Crabb tried to hang on to the tiller as his gondola sped down the twisting, churning waters of the slide. His gondola slammed one side, then the other, and he couldn't seem to control it.

Before long, they were heading toward the right- and left-hand paths.

"Crabb can't control that thing!" Joseph cried. "He'll have to take the children's path, and then we'll have him at the underground dock."

Instead, Crabb rose on wobbly legs, the map box still under his arm, and leaned all his weight into the tiller. He slammed against the far right-hand wall and was knocked to the floor of his gondola. The map box flew into the water.

Then the box floated left, down the children's path, while the gondola with Crabb inside it sailed down the right-hand path. He was heading for the more dangerous route—the one that led to Lower Thunder Falls!

"Forget the box!" cried Fleetfeet.

"What are you saying?!" exclaimed Teegan.

But Joseph's gaze met Fleetfeet's. Both boys now understood what was more important than "winning" their quest.

"I'm with you, claw-brother!" Joseph cried.

"But—"

"Teegan, you jump out up ahead and swim left," advised Fleetfeet. "You should be able to find help to fish out the map box."

"The water's shallow," called Joseph to Teegan. "You can easily swim to the dock."

"Yes," said Fleetfeet. "Joseph and I need to work as a close team to save Crabb now."

Teegan's eyes widened, barely able to believe that these were the same bickering boys she'd met a few days ago. They now appeared to be determined young men.

Without argument she jumped out of the raft and began swimming, taking the "Children and Hatchlings" route to the left and the dock beyond.

Joseph and Fleetfeet guided their raft to the right

and into a channel where they'd never gone before.

"'Here it comes," Joseph said.

"Ready or not!" Fleetfeet cried.

And suddenly they were on the harsh, treacherous waters leading to the falls. Ahead, Crabb's gondola was slamming one side of the rough channel then the other. There was no sign of Crabb inside.

"He must have been knocked out," Fleetfeet called, keeping the craft steady with his oar. Joseph used another oar at the front.

"Hard right!" Joseph cried. "Hard right coming!"

Working as a team, the two expertly guided the raft through the upcoming twists and turns of the chute.

With each sharp turn, the boys found themselves moving down toward a level lower than the turn before. This multi-level, zigzag design had been created to control the incredible speed of the water's rapid downward movement. But, even so, the water was still flowing very swiftly!

Crabb's gondola was in bad shape. Again and again it slammed into the sides of the chutes, bits of the craft flying off.

"It'll be smashed to pieces before we even reach the falls," Joseph said. "I have to get on board to help Crabb!"

"How?" Fleetfeet said. "We can't catch up…wait, I think I know a way," he added, looking down at the level right below them, where Crabb's gondola was about to appear. "It'll be dangerous, but—"

"It's already dangerous," Joseph cried. "Tell me your plan!"

Fleetfeet said, "There's no time. You'll just have to trust me!"

"Always, claw-brother. Always!"

"Get ready to jump!" Fleetfeet said.

"Jump?" Joseph asked. "Where?"

Then he saw it. Crabb's gondola had rushed so far along the zigzagging chute that it was now down on the level directly below them.

Fleetfeet grabbed the back of Joseph's shirt, and together they jumped from their water craft down to Crabb's!

They landed in a heap, smack in the middle of Crabb's gondola. Joseph looked down at the unconscious Lee Crabb. Then he looked over the side of the gondola and saw yet another lower ledge.

Before Joseph knew what was happening, Fleetfeet was calling, "Be ready, Joseph! I'm going to catch you!" Then he jumped into the water below and vanished.

"Fleetfeet!" Joseph cried.

The world lurched as the gondola sank suddenly and spun several times. It was dragged into a darkened cave, where it made a sharp turn and sank downward again as it was thrust into the glaring light of day.

Joseph saw Fleetfeet ahead, one claw and one foot

dug into the rocky side of the mountain. His other claw was outstretched.

Hauling Crabb onto his back, Joseph balanced as well as he could on the out-of-control gondola. It slammed a bank and knocked him flat. He rose on shaking legs and reached up blindly, spray stinging his eyes, the roar of the water drowning out all other sounds.

Then he felt Fleetfeet's powerfully strong claw closing on his arm. He grabbed hold and his friend hauled him and his burden from the gondola just before it flew over the edge and down Lower Thunder Falls.

Their own raft came next, slamming the rocks near them and almost making Fleetfeet lose his grip. But the saurian held on. Soon they found a ledge where they could wait to be rescued.

Help arrived immediately, thanks to Teegan's quick work. A long-necked dinosaur lowered a cart down to them. They climbed upon it and were raised up to the Rosy Morning Promenade, where Teegan waited.

Healers came to tend to Crabb and check on the boys.

"I think you both should read this," Teegan said, handing them a large, thick piece of parchment paper.

"What is it?"

"I was able to retrieve the box that Crabb had been carrying. *This* was inside!"

Joseph took it. Fleetfeet looked at it over his friend's shoulder.

There was a map here, but it was hard to make out. Someone had written a bright red message across the parchment:

IT'S OVER, LADS. COME HOME.

CHAPTER 16

Joseph and Fleetfeet stood before Steelgaze. He lay across his resting chair, snoring. Only two attendants were with him now: the fiery-haired woman named Leonora and one of the Ovinutrix.

Joseph shifted his weight from one leg to another. His hands were clasped behind his back. He stared at the ceiling, making little sighs of frustration and concern.

Fleetfeet wasn't handling the waiting any better. He kept clicking his claws in rhythm to an old song that he played over and over in his head. Soon his tail was tapping, as well.

"Stop that," Leonora said, smiling and shaking her head. "Can't you lads sit still?"

"Might help if we had chairs," Joseph said.

"And keep your voice down," said Leonora. "No need to wake him till all the guests arrive."

"Yes, we certainly don't want old jolly-head any crankier than he normally is," the ostrich-sized saurian beside her said with a laugh.

Joseph leaned in close to his friend. "Guests? What's she talking about?"

"I don't know," replied Fleetfeet.

Just then, the door behind them opened. Joseph and Fleetfeet were startled to see Townsend enter the room—with Lee Crabb. Teegan MacGregor came in behind them.

"Teegan, what's going on?" Joseph asked.

Fleetfeet reeled. "Was Townsend working with Crabb after all?"

"You're about to find out, just like I did," she said with a wink as the men went to Steelgaze.

"About time," the Kentrosaurus said, his eyes still shut, his tail lolling from side to side.

"I think that's our cue," Leonora said, nodding to the Ovinutrix.

The ostrich-sized dinosaur yawned. "He really is cute as can be, isn't he?" the Ovinutrix teased.

"Fah! Away with you both!" Steelgaze roared. "The only reason I've built up my strength is so that I won't have the likes of you fawning over me day and night!"

"See, I told you it would work," said Leonora.

The Ovinutrix's laughter echoed as they left.

Lee Crabb grinned. "How are you, clodhopper?"

"Less grizzled and ornery than *you*," Steelgaze replied.

"Well," Crabb said, "you have room for improvement, then, don't you?"

"Lucky for you I have strong scales," Steelgaze said.

"Ha!" shot back Crabb. "What you really mean is that it's lucky for me that you're stuck in that chair."

"Too true," Steelgaze said. He laughed.

Joseph's and Fleetfeet's jaws dropped at the same time.

"Steelgaze laughed," Joseph whispered. "He laughed and joked with Lee Crabb."

"Thank you. I was worried I was imagining things," Fleetfeet said.

Townsend stepped forward. "You did well, lads." He shifted his gaze to Steelgaze. "But *I'm* not the person you need to hear that from."

Steelgaze looked almost sheepish. "I was just getting to that," the dinosaur said, raising one paw and swiping back and forth with his tail.

"We missed you," Joseph blurted out. He was so surprised by all he was witnessing that he really didn't quite know what to say.

"Yes," Fleetfeet added.

"And I missed you," Steelgaze said. "Both of you. Come closer. You're among friends."

Joseph's confused gaze went to Crabb.

"Yes, even me," Crabb said with a howling laugh. "Ah, for a cigar."

"I suppose I should start at the beginning," Steelgaze said. "Joseph, Fleetfeet, in many ways, you are two of my best, two of my *brightest* students. But it seemed there was one thing I couldn't teach you. And that was how to work together."

"But—you always made us compete," Fleetfeet said.

"No," Steelgaze said. "I put you in competition. I didn't *make* you compete. There's a difference. Just like that saying you two always threw at one another: *Fair is the advantage to those who possess it.* You never did understand what that saying really meant, my boys: One may call an advantage fair simply because he has it—but that doesn't make the advantage truly fair, or right."

Joseph felt a redness creep into his cheeks. Fleetfeet's gaze dropped. Both boys had been so busy using the words to justify themselves in contests that they'd never stopped to consider their true meaning.

"You see," continued Steelgaze, "my hope was that when each of you tried so hard to outdo the other, that you'd find it inside yourselves to strive for heights of achievement you might not have reached otherwise. And I believe that happened, time and again. But there were even greater heights for each of you to reach that had nothing to do with prizes or praise.

"Inside each of our hearts, lads, are goals unique to us. Only our hearts can tell us what these special goals are. But you two had not yet learned how to listen to your hearts."

Joseph hung his head. "I'm sorry we let you down."

"Fah! You are misunderstanding me. Joseph, you and Fleetfeet are kind and gentle souls, adventurous and high-spirited. You are both very devoted to the Dinotopian ideals, but you are also young and head-strong. You have been so eager to *hear* approval echoing in your *ears* that you never stopped to *listen* for it in your own *hearts.*"

The Kentrosaurus paused a moment to see if his words were finally being understood by the boys—and not simply heard. When he was satisfied, he continued.

"Each of you needed to learn this valuable lesson of knowing how to listen to your hearts. I knew you both enjoyed competitions, so I devised one last contest for you.

"Competition, lads, can be healthy, but never at the cost of a higher good. So, the only way either of you could have won my competition was if you discovered *from your own hearts,* what was the higher good."

"The map," Joseph said. "Lee Crabb didn't take it so that he could turn a profit—"

Fleetfeet jumped in. "He was a *part* of this whole chase, from the beginning!"

"And so was Townsend," added Joseph.

Lee Crabb turned to Steelgaze. "They ain't so slow as you'd think, eh?"

"Indeed," Steelgaze said. "The map wasn't real.

137

But the journey's dangers were. That's why I asked my friend Townsend to keep a careful eye on the whole affair."

"True enough," said Crabb. "And I was only too happy to sign on after Steelgaze offered to pay me in valuable barter. Besides, it sounded like rippin' good fun!"

"Townsend agreed to help because he was once *my* mentor," Steelgaze said.

"I was happy to help," said Townsend.

"So," said Joseph, gathering his courage, "have we passed the test?"

"What do you think?" asked Steelgaze. "Have you learned the value of working together? Have you learned how to hear what is right—not through your ears, but through your own hearts?"

Joseph and Fleetfeet looked at one another. Then they both smiled, hearing the answer loud and clear in their *hearts*. They both felt proud of their efforts and their actions. And they both knew they'd discovered important things about themselves along the way.

"Good," said Steelgaze, seeing the understanding in the boys' faces. "Now the two of you must let me rest. But don't tell Leonora and her friend what I'm up to. They'll want to come back in and fuss all over me."

The boys and Teegan were just about to leave the chamber when Steelgaze called, "Joseph, Fleetfeet!"

The boys turned.

"I just wanted to say that *I'm* proud to have had you as students."

The boys nodded, their faces barely able to contain the width of their grins. They left the chamber and headed down a long hallway.

"Well, boys, that was fun!" exclaimed Teegan.

Joseph turned to her. "I'm glad you were entertained," he said with a laugh. "So, what are *you* going to do now?"

"Don't worry about me," she said as they approached the house's large entryway. "Townsend said that he'd help me. I have to begin my schooling, after all. But what about you two? Seems to me that you've just graduated."

"I've decided that I'd like to become a teacher," Joseph said. "Like Steelgaze."

"And you, Fleetfeet?" Teegan asked.

"I'd like to go back to those ruins. There are secrets in the past that might help us today. And I'd like to find them."

Teegan smiled. "Well, before each of my gallant, errant knights embarks on his grand destiny, do you think either of you might be up for a little race? A friendly competition?"

"Well," Joseph said. "I really should go to the library. There's a lot I have to learn if I want to be a teacher like Steelgaze."

Fleetfeet nodded. "And I must find a seeker of the past who'll teach me the proper ways of unearthing and restoring its treasures."

"Don't work too hard, my friends," Teegan said. "It seems to me that you're already learning."

Then they left Steelgaze's house and walked down the street together, their spirits blazing brighter than the noonday sun.

ABOUT THE AUTHOR

SCOTT CIENCIN, a best-selling author of juvenile and adult fiction, has been praised by *Science Fiction Review* as "one of today's finest fantasy writers." In addition to *Thunder Falls,* Scott has also written two other Dinotopia novels for Random House: *Windchaser* and *Lost City.*

"I grew up with a love of the fantastic," said Scott. "Being given the opportunity to write novels set in the world of James Gurney's Dinotopia put me on a path of discovery...In creating Dinotopia, James Gurney became the heir to the legacy of Jules Verne and other classic fantasists. Having the opportunity to add to the mythology he's created has not only made me a better writer, it's taught me lessons about the limitless vistas of the imagination."

Among Scott Ciencin's many other works are *Godzilla: King of the Monsters, The Ways of Magic,* and the on-line Internet series "The Lurker Files," now published in book form. Scott is also working on his own original comic book series for DC Comics.

HATCHLING
By Midori Snyder

Janet is thrilled when she is made an apprentice at the Hatchery, the place where dinosaur eggs are taken care of. But the first time she has to watch over the eggs at night, she falls asleep. When she wakes up, one of the precious dinosaur eggs has a crack in it—a crack that could prove fatal to the baby dinosaur within.

Afraid of what people will think, Janet runs away to find a place where no one knows of her mistake. Instead, she finds Kranog, a wounded Hadrosaur. Kranog is trying to return to the abandoned city of her birth to lay her egg, but she can't do it without Janet's help. Now Janet will have to face her fears about both the journey ahead and herself.

LOST CITY
By Scott Ciencin

In search of adventure, thirteen-year-old Andrew convinces his friends, Lian and Ned, to explore the forbidden Lost City of Dinotopia. But the last thing they expect to discover is a group of meat-eating Troodons!

For centuries, this lost tribe of dinosaurs has lived secretly in the crumbling city. Now Andrew and his friends are trapped. They must talk the tribe into joining the rest of Dinotopia. Otherwise, the Troodons may try to protect their secrets by making Andrew, Ned, and Lian citizens of the Lost City—for good!

SABERTOOTH MOUNTAIN
By John Vornholt

For years, sabertooth tigers have lived in the Forbidden Mountains, apart from humans and dinosaurs alike. Now an avalanche has blocked their way to their source of food, and the sabertooths are divided on what to do. The only hope for a peaceful solution lies with Redstripe, a sabertooth leader, and Cai, a thirteen-year-old boy. This unlikely pair embarks on a treacherous journey out of the mountains. But they are only a few steps ahead of a human-hating sabertooth and his hungry followers—in a race that could change Dinotopia forever.

And coming in June 1997...

FIRESTORM
By Gene DeWeese

Olivia, Albert, and their dinosaur partners want to be chosen as apprentices to the Habitat Partners of the Forest. But first they must face the dangers and adventures of the Dinotopian jungle!

REVIST THE WORLD OF

DINOTOPIA

in these titles,
available wherever books are sold...

OR

You can send in this coupon (with check or money order)
and have the books mailed directly to you!

☐ ***Windchaser*** (0-679-86981-6) $3.99
by Scott Ciencin

☐ ***River Quest*** (0-679-86982-4) $3.99
by John Vornholt

☐ ***Hatchling*** (0-679-86984-0) $3.99
by Midori Snyder

☐ ***Lost City*** (0-679-86983-2) $3.99
by Scott Ciencin

☐ ***Sabertooth Mountain*** (0-679-88095-X) $3.99
by John Vornholt

☐ ***Thunder Falls*** (0-679-88256-1) $3.99
by Scott Ciencin

Subtotal . . . . $ _____
Shipping and handling . . . . $ _3.00_
Sales tax (where applicable) . . . . $ _____
Total amount enclosed . . . . $ _____

Name _____

Address _____

City _____ State _____ Zip _____

Make your check or money order (no cash or C.O.D.s)
payable to Random House and mail to:
Bullseye Mail Sales, 400 Hahn Road, Westminster, MD 21157.

Prices and numbers subject to change without notice. Valid in U.S. only.
All orders subject to availability. Please allow 4 to 6 weeks for delivery.

Need your books even faster? Call toll-free 1-800-793-2665
to order by phone and use your major credit card.
Please mention interest code 049-20 to expedite your order.